SABINA QUARTET

SABINA QUARTET

G. D. Spilsbury

BERGAMOT

Bergamot Books
bergamotbooks.com

ISBN 978-1-7354275-5-3

For Phil Trupp

It is no small thing to live the entire day face to face with all three hundred and sixty degrees of this panorama. It is necessary to be well trained and fortified in spirit to be able to bear it. But, if one can manage it, one can acquire at times the illusion of fitting like the right piece, even if cut imperfectly, into the great universal puzzle, and of perceiving something of the mysterious design that holds it all together.

—Raffaele La Capria

SABINA QUARTET

KEEPER OF
MONTE DONATO

A busy Saturday lay ahead, with a dinner party in the evening, but Julie Barrett's early morning began with her usual homage to the valley that spread with divine beauty before her hilltop home. Soft rosy colors tingled over the ancient hills and distant mountains. The air was pure and cleansing, and the gentle silence was broken only by a cock's crow or a dog's bark. Peace reigned everywhere, even though farming life was toil. Nature, ever present, ever showing its beauty, was a constant reward, a balm of love and hope for the spirit. And the olive trees—they were like household pets needing constant attention and care. They were small and cheerful-looking and the black and green fruit they produced each autumn was pure gold to human life.

Julie, an American artist, had been living in the Sabina hills for almost a year, learning the new terrain, a farming way of life. For twenty-five hundred years the rugged slopes and winding valleys capped by medieval hilltowns had been supplying Rome with handmade olive oil. Each day dawned with the land waiting for the farm work that lay ahead, from the seasonal harvesting, pruning, and haying to the ordinary chores of feeding and slaughtering the animals. Julie tended the olives on her property—she had just completed her first harvest—and the rest of the time she painted.

Greeting her landscape that Saturday morning, feeling its pulse of life and expectation, she couldn't help but compare it to the night, when darkness brought mystery to the mountain, her mountain. As she went from door to door, locking all the shutters, she would take a last look at the stars. They hung so close, as if part of her yard, an animate and friendly force. The last door was upstairs in her studio and faced the driveway's plateau, for the house clung to Monte Donato's steep slope. On moonlit nights the mountain's white rocks rising above the sandy driveway glowed with an extra-terrestrial luminescence, like an eerie planet. Her occasional dinner guests invariably asked, "How can you stand it here? It's spooky." But it was only spooky at night when all the shutters were locked and the downstairs echoed like a strange chamber. The previous owners had transformed the rustic dwelling into a contemporary villetta. The lower level—once a stall for a few animals and storage space for implements and food—was now a spacious kitchen and living room. An original cave could be accessed through a modern sliding door next to the staircase. The upstairs had three bedrooms, and the one that opened to the driveway now served as Julie's studio. Many of her neighbors still lived above their animals, although just as many had sold olive groves to pay for modernizations, including household bathrooms.

Julie knew where Monte Donato's nocturnal eeriness came from. It was the mountain and what it contained in its summit only seventy yards from her door—a giant necropolis from the hilltown's destruction in 1307. The lives lost there remained present, as memory, the way any site involving a massacre remained. She had explored the ruins and cleared some of the hunters' overgrown trails winding through them. With Riccardo's help, she had chain-sawed a thicket of saplings at the summit to open up a view of Collediana, the neighboring hilltown and local municipal government, and also the ancient rival and destroyer of Monte Donato. The best pieces of stone and marble had long since been carted off to adorn the victor's walls, but Monte Donato's tragic foundations remained and at night seemed to seep into the air surrounding the mountain.

Julie had come to the Sabina a year after the death of her husband, Alan, from prostate cancer. He had been forty-seven. In college, she had studied art in Florence and he architecture in Rome. They had always dreamed of living in Italy again. Their only child, Annie, had finished graduate school and was teaching high-school math in New York. Julie found herself free to roam. Old friends from her year abroad had urged her to look at the Sabina, where rural property was still affordable. By luck she had become the owner of Monte Donato and took on the new sideline of tending olives. In no time it became apparent that her new home, at least at night, felt like the lone survivor of the mountain's silent grave.

With a twinge of regret, Julie concluded her early morning ritual of landscape-gazing and turned back to the kitchen to start the water for tea. The day ahead was tightly scheduled. A stonemason was coming by to give her an estimate for a retaining wall on her lower level, and nineteen-year-old Riccardo was planning to finish the rough-hewn staircase he was building to access the new kitchen garden. In the afternoon, Julie would get started on her dinner. She had invited William, Colin, and Sylvia. They were all from Britain, though Sylvia, Colin's wife, was Italian-born. Julie had met them a few times at ex-pat gatherings and thought they might be potential friends. They all liked to read and had interesting hobbies—William was restoring a fabulous apartment he had bought for a song. It was the first floor of a sixteenth-century palace. The stone floors tilted and the long row of windows passing through room after room rose from floor to ceiling, offering sublime views of sunsets over the rolling hills. Old frescoes covered the walls, which he had touched up himself, matching the colors. In the wintertime, he lived in two rooms where he had installed woodburning stoves, for the rest of the house was *gelato*, freezing. He frequently entertained, for he loved to share his setting and explain his latest renovation, work he did himself, often on his back from scaffolding. Art was his hobby but he also read literature and liked to talk about it. He gave English lessons in Rome to lawyers and politicians. Colin and Sylvia had recently organized an outing club and liked cultural activities. Socially the Sabina hills had protocols: first and foremost, Italian families socialized with their own families. Farmers rarely mixed with ex-pats or educated Italians from Rome, or locals who got educated in Rome and returned to build pretentious villas on the family property, often just a few yards from the humble stone dwellings used for centuries. The nobility mixed with other nobility and occasionally with grammar-school friends who weren't aristocrats. They also dined with selected ex-pats. Ex-pats did the most socializing, frequenting Bar Luna along a cobbled lane in Collediana and while there making dates for future get-togethers. Among this group were foreign-born spouses married to Italians from the professional class.

Julie had invited some of her farming neighbors over for dinner but soon discovered this was not typical for them, partly because they had so many feuds going that they were reluctant to come in case one of their enemies was on the guest list. Additionally, lunch was their main meal eaten at home. At night, exhausted from farm work, they went to bed early, except for the young folk, who went out cavorting.

Julie finished her tea just as Riccardo's noisy Vespa sounded in the driveway above. She slipped into shoes and went out to greet him. He was young and wiry and she loved looking at his nimble figure with its long neck that grew right into his shapely head as if carved from a single tree trunk. Black curly hair, black rounded eyebrows, liquid brown eyes with sweeping black lashes, and a resplendent smile—he couldn't have looked more enticingly Mediterranean. He had quit school after eighth grade and contributed to the family household through a variety of part-time jobs.

They spoke Italian; few farmers spoke English.

"Julie," he gave her perfunctory kisses on each cheek. "Do you want my horses to graze here this spring?"

"Yes."

"Good, then I'll be setting up my ropes in the next few weeks."

Throughout the neighboring fields, he cordoned off swaths of land for the horses to graze and to keep them away from people's homes. The horses munched down the wild spring growth in the orchards and left manure behind. Everyone benefited. Sometimes the horses escaped and then the buzz went out to find Riccardo, who eventually appeared on the scene to corral them. Riccardo adored horses and trained them for other people; he also competed throughout Italy and won trophies. One of Julie's first experiences in the Sabina involved Riccardo and his horses. His family lived in the valley below her, and one evening as she took a long walk along the road that passed his house, a sudden and terrifying thunder under her feet made her leap to the side. And just in time, for a dark, wild horseman galloped by, yelping his round-up calls and waving a short rope in the sky. A dozen horses stampeded behind him, heading home to the stall from someone's pasture. In the rear, Riccardo's little beagle-mutt galloped for all his short legs would allow, barking ferociously like the sergeant in charge.

Now, with dexterous speed Riccardo was rolling a barrel of gravel over to the new staircase. Julie followed. In stages, he had cut down and stripped thin trees from her hill to make poles for the structure. Between each wide and disproportionately steep step he had packed loose stones from the yard. Gravel was the finishing touch. Julie looked down at his hand-hewn staircase. The descent couldn't look more dangerous for the hips. But it was authentic, rural handiwork passed down through the ages, an innate knowledge. "I really like it, Riccardo, thank you."

"I'm going to finish today. I'm sorry it took so long but I had other work and it was hard to dig here. Your land is *roccioso*—all rock That's why none of us one would ever live here."

"But the olive oil is good."

"The best. But you have no water, you have no soil, and you're on a cliff." He poured gravel over the top step and crouched to spread it.

"I've been thinking about all the rocks," Julie said, joining him to rake the pebbles with her fingers. "Not just the big ones but all the little pieces. They're like a ground cover of broken china."

He clicked his teeth, "*Esatto,*" exactly.

"Do you think it's the old hilltown's rubble that slowly got crushed over centuries and slid down the mountain?"

He paused, considering. "No, it's just rocky, that's all."

She sighed in disappointment, for she wanted answers for the way things were on Monte Donato, and unusually rocky soil was one of its features. Early on Riccardo had walked her land with her, showing her the ancient paths. He knew every inch of the property from riding his horses on the trails and from being an avid hunter in the thickets. And his senses were keen to nature. Once, when the two of them walked down the driveway in the dark to his uncle Mario's house, his arms had suddenly plunged into a shrub and returned with a baby porcupine. That was Riccardo, a nineteen-year-old gifted in the ways of nature and the land.

The stonemason, Martoni, came by after Riccardo left. He was a handsome man in fancier clothes than the farmers and he drove a new SUV. He inspected the kitchen's patio that needed a retaining wall, and then walked around the rest of the house telling Julie other places she could add walls and contrived paths for a true villa look. By the time they finished their tour, she knew nothing would ever happen with him. He had different ideas from her, grandiose, tacky schemes, and she knew his bid for the only job she needed done—the wall—would come in sky high. But she smiled politely and thanked him before he left.

No sooner had the dust settled from his exiting vehicle than her neighbor Mario's old black pick-up roared into the drive and he slammed out of the cab.

"Julie, that man is *cattivo*, bad!" he exclaimed, almost spitting out his dentures, his hand flying to their rescue. "Don't let him do any work for you! He'll rob you! He's a *ladro*, thief!"

"Okay, don't worry, he won't do any work here. I assure you."

Mario wiped his brow, his tension easing. He always spoke fast and munched back his words so that often they were unintelligible. "Listen, Julie, just tell me what work you want done and I'll tell you who to call."

"*Bene,*" she answered.

He pointed at her scissors, "What are you doing?"

"I was going to pick flowers—some friends are coming over for dinner."

"I'll help you."

He strolled with her to the upper olive grove and pointed out the flowers she should cut—red nuggets of once blooming wild roses, sprigs of purple *mentuccia,* a wild mint, and white shepherd's purse. It pleased her that Mario took such an interest in helping her gather the bouquet. He had found a stick and was sweeping through the rough grass to find buds or leaves of interest. When her foot got tangled in a nasty vine he laughed, "*Caccia braghe!* trouser catchers," and took her scissors to cut her loose.

Mario was her self-appointed protector. He was a short, strong Roman in his mid-seventies and dyed his hair a sandy brown, for he still went dancing every Saturday night and liked to appear debonair to the ladies. He was her nearest neighbor down the road and could see every car that went up her driveway. Often he phoned her to ask if the strange car that had just paid her a visit was someone she knew. When she drove past his house she often saw him doing chores in his courtyard and stopped to call hello through her window. He liked to come to the gate to chat for a few minutes, always reminding her how he was watching over her. He was a widower and had inherited hundreds of hectares of valuable olive land from his wife Celestina. As most farmers in the valley were intermarried, they resented Mario for owning their blood relative's land, mainly because he was from Rome—an outsider, the ancient enemy. From the days of the Sabina women's kidnapping by the Romans, the two cultures had been archrivals. Because Mario and Celestina had been childless—she was fifteen years older than he—they had lavished all their love and resources on Riccardo, her youngest nephew, and one day he would inherit all of Mario's possessions. "He is like my own son," Mario often told Julie. And from local whisperings she had learned that Riccardo really was his son by Celestina's cousin, Angela.

With flowers in hand, they headed back to the driveway. Walking the steep grade of the upper olive grove had winded Mario. He was getting old even if he looked robust. Farming broke the body. His swollen hands no longer moved easily and harvesting his olives took several months. Riccardo and another young recruit helped when they could, but Riccardo's other jobs took most of his time. As soon as Julie had finished her own modest harvest—twenty-five liters of oil—she had helped Mario by cleaning leaves and twigs from his fruit before the laden crates went off to the mill. Those hours working together in his courtyard had been happily spent talking about their lives and the Sabina's nature. From Mario Julie had learned how to hunt wild asparagus, which sprouted up in the spring like filigree ferns next to rocks and tree trunks. They were hard to spot, but Julie had soon caught on to their camouflaging habits and proudly displayed a large handful to Mario. He had taken it home only to return at lunchtime with a warm asparagus frittata in a frying pan covered with a dishtowel.

In the countryside the seasons revolved around food, what could be harvested and prepared. Mario had taught her how to make *carciofi alla romana,* Roman artichokes, seasoned with the mentuccia in her yard. He had helped her plant a lemon tree and an essential *alloro* bush, for many recipes called for fresh bay. Along her driveway wall she had planted other herbs—*salvia, timo, maggiorana.* That autumn, Mario had also taken her to the best spot for picking blackberries. Together they had filled three baskets, from which she made jam and gave him half. When she went back on her own for another basket, the hunters were out and the gunshots whistled by, so she sang *April, Come She Will,* over and over again as she picked, never quite overcoming her tension that she might be mistaken for a rustling bird in the blackberry patch.

The one hunting expedition Mario never took her on was for *tartufi,* truffles. His freezer was full of the black gold. Restaurants paid hundreds of euros for this delicacy. He had trained one of his dogs to hunt the black wrinkled nuggets. He did this by making a ball that he coated with tartufi. As the puppy matured, Mario kept tossing him the ball to fetch. By the time the pup was ready for hunting, the only scent he would fight to the death for was tartufo. Mario made *fettuccine al tartufo* for Julie several times but never took her hunting for the rare mushroom and probably for two reasons: first, no one ever revealed where they hunted tartufi because it was an extremely competitive activity (the wild boars also routed for it); second, such competition could be dangerous. Someone had slashed Mario's tires because he was hunting in territory they considered their own. Who could trust what other crimes might result over the coveted treasure? After all, everyone carried rifles, and this was Italy.

Despite their camaraderie, Julie and Mario rarely ate dinner together because—as Mario gestured with a swirl of his head for the surrounding countryside—neighbors would talk. And gossip was rampant, much of it invented. The few times they did eat together, Mario was far more comfortable if Julie came to his house, and possibly because he liked his own superior cooking. He came from a family of restaurant owners and had worked in kitchens from the age of five. When he came to her house, washed and combed, he sat stiffly, formally, and left as soon as he could.

With a sigh of reluctance to return to the work-a-day world, Mario opened his truck door. "Oh yes, this is for you," he said, reaching in and pulling a bag from the passenger seat. More fresh eggs. He often brought them.

"Thank you."

"I can't eat them, too much cholesterol," he reminded her. "I feed them to the dogs."

A green tractor ground into the driveway alongside Mario's truck. At the helm, high above them, was handsome Alberto, one of Collediana's most respected farmers because of his unparalleled energy for work, almost a mania. He had cut Julie's overgrown grass in the orchards the past summer, letting her know with his white-toothed grin how lucky she was because no one else would risk their tractors or their lives to mow that steep rocky slope.

But now his face was livid. "I won't do any more work for you if Martoni works here!" he roared.

"I already told her," Mario shouted back.

"That *stronzo,* asshole, lives right next to me and one day I'm going to kill him."

"Don't worry," Julie said, "Martoni is not going to work here."

"He's a thief," Mario shrilled.

"Good, because I'll never come back if he does," Alberto repeated, locking his arms over his chest, his blue eyes bright with emotion.

"It's all settled, Martoni's not working here," Julie repeated with a warm smile that assured Alberto of her loyalty. "Would you like a coffee?"

"Grazie." His gentlemanly courtesy returned immediately and he tipped his cap with a rakish grin.

There was no way Mario—who never drank coffee after his morning demitasse—was going to leave Julie alone with such a rival. Readily he accepted her invitation to join them, and the three neighbors set off for the kitchen, Julie in the middle and fully aware that in real life the two men never spoke to each other.

The sun was long down and the temperature had dropped to the low fifties by the eight o'clock dinner hour. The outside lights were on, and except for cooking the pasta, Julie's dinner was ready.

From the downstairs kitchen, she heard car doors slam and cheery voices in the driveway. Bundled up against the chill, Sylvia, Colin, and William came down the curving brick steps to the kitchen door, which Julie already held open. Sylvia's voice pealed out, "But shouldn't we stop to look at this view before we go in, or would that be rude?"

Arms offered gifts of wine, homemade jam, home-cured olives, and a *crostata* tart, the popular local dessert. Colin towered over the rest of them like an awkward schoolboy, only now gray and grizzled with unruly hair and a beard that looked as though it collected everything. A good-humored laugh throttled in his throat much of the time, as if a nervous tic. His wife Sylvia's shock of white hair and large, gold-framed glasses magnified her intense face and the wide smile sewn to her ears even when she expressed outrage. She was from Padua and spoke English loudly and correctly as if pounding in her words with a hammer to prove her mastery of the language. William was soft and refined, with thinning gray hair combed neatly over his pate and a bulbous nose with broken veins. He dressed conservatively in corduroy slacks, a sweater, and tasseled shoes.

Julie led them to the echoing living room where she had set up hors d'oeuvres. William took charge of pouring wine as Julie asked Sylvia about her life.

"I was an importer of Indian textiles," Sylvia said crisply.

"I didn't know that," William said. "I always thought you taught English."

"I did teach English, but only on the side, at the Italian cultural center. My main career was in textiles."

"How did you two meet?" Julie asked.

"It's a long story," Sylvia answered. "I left Italy when I was eighteen to seek my fortune. I was an adventuress, you see. I was appalled at the mold my parents had planned for me, and I took off. I traveled to India, got involved with merchants, and eventually I was running my own business in London, where

I met Colin. And believe me, this was no small business, I was the principal textile supplier throughout the UK. When Colin announced he wanted early retirement two years ago, I more than cheered the motion—in fact, I was the one who made it happen. He's the type who would sit around wanting to do something but never taking the necessary steps to make it happen. Not me, I'm just the opposite. Action is my middle name!" She brandished her smile like a gleaming sword.

Julie asked Colin about his former work.

"Can't you tell by looking at him what kind of work he did?" Sylvia said.

"I'm a geek," Colin chuckled, saving Sylvia from saying it.

"Colin has six or seven patents for software, and not unimportant ones either, mind you."

"Six is correct," Colin confirmed. "But I'm done with that. I'm into studying the stars now."

"You're not kidding, he practically broke the bank buying himself a fancy telescope," Sylvia said.

Colin's chuckle rattled in his throat.

William topped off their wine glasses, and in his lilting voice described the Roman aristocrats he met every week for English conversation. "And it's damn good pay," he said. "Besides that, I like the contact. I go to their palaces and sit in their elegantly furnished drawing rooms, with papal portraits of their relatives, and enjoy lively discussion on Italian politics and history, while a servant in livery delivers us coffee in one-hundred-year-old china cups. We become friends. In fact, one of my clients is coming out to see my place tomorrow—he might buy it."

"What? You're selling already?" Sylvia said.

"If I get the price I want, yes, and then I'd buy three smaller places, fix them up, and so on."

"But that's your home," Julie said. "Don't you want to enjoy the place you've fixed up with your own hands?"

"No, not really, I don't feel attachments like that. I just like fixing up the place and finding a buyer. Despite my English blood, I'm an American at heart." He laughed lightly, "And to be quite honest, I wouldn't be opposed at all to living in America—I've given it quite a bit of thought."

Sylvia's eyes were roving about the living room, as if to understand why it sounded like a dark, hollow chamber. "I say, Julie, don't you feel isolated here?"

"No. My neighbors come around to help with the yard work and I can walk to town."

"Yes, but I mean at night. It's so dark and solitary here—don't you get spooked? I mean especially as a woman?"

"No," Julie said, even though she did feel vulnerable at night when the silent necropolis above her house breathed with its own mysterious and invisible life. Indoors, her cavernous downstairs rooms rested in the pitch black once the shutters were closed. And the cave was there full of its secret movements. The upstairs was cozier and she kept her bedroom shutters open to starlight and moonlight. But wind often tore down the mountains, howling and pummeling the house. It stood like the solid rock it was, but she couldn't help imagining the furious face of the wind god attacking her door. And finally, something she hadn't anticipated when she moved to the Sabina was dealing with men. They often took liberties when they hugged her, squeezing inappropriately— even Mario at first. Some made suggestive remarks that were inappropriate. Thus, she had become wary of men in general, which increased her sense of vulnerability at night in her dark house on its solitary hillside. What if a man suddenly burst in? Sometimes, when she couldn't fall asleep, she got up and locked her bedroom door.

"Well, good luck to you, personally I couldn't do it," Sylvia said.

"I love it," Julie assured her. "Hey, I'd better start the pasta so we can eat."

"Let me help," Colin said, his long legs leaping to action.

"He can be a good helper in the kitchen," Sylvia's voice trailed after them.

The water was already simmering in the pot. Julie turned up the flame and added the rigatoni. Then she turned on the burner under the sauce, while Colin's tall shadow dodged around her.

"How did your Italian get so good? Do you speak it at home?"

"No," he said. "But before we bought our house here, Sylvia and I had been coming to Italy for vacations for thirty years. After the first few trips I knew I couldn't continue if I didn't master the language, so I took off six months from work and studied in Bologna."

"Mmm, I'd like to do that some day, or is it too late?"

"It's never too late—studying languages is one of the best exercises for the mind."

"But for now, I don't want to live in Bologna for six months."

"You could commute to Perugia."

"Yes, except I want to spend every day here."

"Me too, that's why we've organized the Sunday excursions—to really explore this part of Italy."

"It's a great idea and I plan to join some of them." She held out a rigatoni on the end of her pasta spoon, "Here, do you want to do the taste test?"

"No, not me, that's too big a responsibility in this country."

"But we're all foreigners—or I guess Sylvia isn't—she just sounds British."

"She's very British. But also knows where the living is good, even though we never stop marveling at the total inefficiency of this country. Don't you find it frustrating when you set out to accomplish the most simple task and all you meet are insurmountable obstacles, some of them invented randomly on the spot?"

"Oh, yes, all the time, but then I go out for lunch with friends and I'm glad I'm here."

"It's all about the food, isn't it? That's the pivotal point in this culture."

"Yes, but you have to throw in the scenery and the art and the history, because the food gets linked to that, even if it's just a walk after the meal that passes a ruin or an amazing abbey. Or, it could be the table talk about traditions, or the setting of the meal itself, in an ancient grotto decorated with medieval implements."

"That's what it is, that's why we're here."

Julie turned off the flame and grabbed the potholders, "It's ready."

"Here, let me do that." He took the pot and drained the pasta in the sink while Julie called the others.

They were all ravenous and ate with relish—rigatoni with broccoli, anchovy, and peperoncino, followed by saltimbocca with pureed potatoes to soak up the savory pan juices. It was creamy, aromatic comfort food, just what Julie had been looking forward to all day. It gratified her to hear satisfied murmurs around the table as the food caressed palates. Dinner talk began with food, the ingredients of the meal and then moved on to recipes, local restaurants, and picturesque places to visit. They all agreed that the Sabina's produce was only average, which was surprising for an agricultural region.

"But not typical agriculture," William said. "They only care about olives here."

"And the younger generation doesn't want to do olives any-more," Julie said.

"Nope, subsistence living went out the window when the EU came in. Anyone ready for more wine?" William asked as he filled his glass.

"Well, you can't blame them, can you?" Sylvia said. "They see all this stuff on TV and they want it too. Why should they slave in the fields like their parents and live in dire poverty when they can sell a few hectares and be rich?"

"It's going to ruin the landscape," Julie said.

"It already has—look what my neighbors did," William said. "That hideous resort sits empty year-round. It'll rot before anyone comes to it. And meanwhile it's spoiled the bucolic beauty that defines this place. It's a crime—the local government still operates in the medieval way and hasn't gotten around to zoning laws."

"They have now," Colin said.

"Well, too late."

"Yes, I daresay it is."

While Julie cleared the plates and brought out dessert, conversation turned to Colin and Sylvia's day tours.

"Sometimes I worry about the ex-pats taking over the Sabina," William said in a lamenting voice as he poured himself yet another glass of wine. "I want to keep the Sabina the way it is, a farming community with a sprinkling of foreigners. Isn't that why we're all here? Why spoil it?"

Sylvia's shoulders drew back in offense, "Are you saying that our monthly tours are threatening the Sabina?"

"It's not meant as a criticism," William said. "I'm just saying I like the Sabina the way it's always been—I've been living here for a decade. I'm one of the first ex-pats. I've seen changes that worry me. Tell me, who signs up for your tours? Ex-pats? That's not intended as a criticism. I'm just trying to state the facts."

Sylvia's voice rang out, partly because of the downstair's echoing power, "Is it my fault that the local people aren't interested in our excursions? We post flyers all over the town giving everyone an equal opportunity to join in. Is it my fault only the ex-pats respond?"

"As I said, I'm not criticizing. I'm just feeling sorry for what's happening here. Everyone's finding out about our hidden paradise. And we're a growing population living separately. I can't say I like it. I want to mix with the real people here."

"And we're not real?" Sylvia gasped. Then the two of them argued in circles about ex-pat activities and how to integrate local people. Colin and Julie occasionally found a crack in the conversation to add something.

"How can you expect the farmers to have the same interests—" Colin started.

Sylvia's invisible fly swatter came down on him, "I never expected my neighbors to sign up for the excursions. The reality is, the people here who are the most like me happen to speak English, and why should we feel frowned upon because we pursue our interests together?"

"I have plenty of friends here who are Italian and not farmers, but they aren't likely to sign up for your tours," William said.

"Give me an example."

"Why, the countess who lives across the piazza from me. We dine together once a week and talk about all kinds of things. Our worlds aren't far apart at all."

"Well good for you, William. And believe me, making friends and connections has never been a problem for me. When I was in business, the phone never stopped ringing. I was the best there was, the best, and everyone wanted me. There was no way I could satisfy the demand. I thanked the heavens when Colin announced he wanted to retire. I was the one needing it more than he!"

"What are your hobbies here?" Julie asked.

Sylvia's gold glasses spun on her, as if she had been attacked from behind, "I keep plenty busy, don't you worry, dearie. My days are so filled I can't get to half the things I planned. I read voraciously, for one, sometimes a book a day."

Colin's throat chuckled, "True."

"Do you know what I'm reading?" William's voice curled through the air to them like a slithering snake.

"Tell me," Sylvia said.

"My favorite author, the Sicilian, Andrea Camilleri."

"I don't know about him, what's he written?"

"He's absolutely the best thing out there and has taken all kinds of prizes. I can't get enough of him. As soon as a new book comes out, I gobble it up, and then have to wait for the next one to be written. He writes hilarious mysteries with the same detective in each, and all in Sicilian dialect. Julie, do you have any grappa?"

Julie went to the cave for the grappa and then took liqueur glasses from the cabinet. She filled William's glass first, and he let the shot slide down his throat, burning hot, before letting out a satisfied exhale.

"And you can understand Sicilian?" Sylvia said.

"Yes, it's no problem for me. You see, I relate to this man as if I were his clone. I want to meet him. And I want to translate him into English, that's my next project. I've already decided to give up my clients in Rome in order to translate Camilleri's books."

"How will you go about that?" Julie asked. "I mean, asking to be his translator. Do you contact his publisher?"

"I don't know, maybe some of you have advice for me. I was thinking of writing Camilleri a letter and telling him I wanted to be his English translator."

"You could include a sample chapter," Sylvia said.

"Good idea."

"Are you sure he hasn't been translated yet if he's won so many prizes?" Julie asked.

William poured another shot of grappa, right to the rim. "All I'm sure of is, the mysterious universe has put the two of us on this planet for a reason: to find each other and collaborate."

"Aren't you worried about driving tonight, William," Sylvia said.

"Not at all. I enjoy drinking and am perfectly willing to risk my life for it."

"It's not your life I was thinking about but the innocent people on the road who might lose their lives when you come around the bend."

"Rubbish."

But the grappa was working its effects on William. Over the course of the evening, he had drunk more than a bottle of wine without showing his inebriation, but with the grappa, his mind began to unravel. He launched into a lamentation about Gretchen, his wealthy New Yorker girlfriend from two years before who had no intention of returning to the Sabina or him.

"I think about her all the time," he said poetically, his body in a state of total relaxation, the paunch upturned, and his left hand lax on the green cashmere sweater draping over it. "I called her today, and do you know where she was? At Tiffany's bar, looking at diamonds." He said this with pride, as if Gretchen's wealth reflected on him, raised his status. "I told her while she sat there: Do you know that I love you?"

"And?" Sylvia's voice bayoneted him from across the table. "Did she respond? Is this relationship really going anywhere, William?"

"Yes, she answered me," William said softly, contritely. "She said she knew it."

"But did she say she loved you?" Sylvia persisted.

William never stirred from his sated repose, except to pour drips of grappa into his glass as if it were an intravenous tube feeding his veins. "You see, you don't understand—you and Colin have it all. You have each other, you're together, you care for one another, but I'm all alone. I'm jealous of you, I really am."

"I wouldn't be too jealous," Sylvia's voice shrilled back. "Colin and I are only lucky we're still together, and don't get me wrong, I love Colin and Colin is all I want, but when the kids left home three years ago, we almost split up. I was ready to divorce him. I looked at this guy and I said, who is this? I don't know him, I don't even like him, I'm outta here! It was hard labor to get us back on track, and even so, I still hate him a lot of the time, he has so many faults, and that's not to say I don't have my own faults, but I'm a lot easier to live with! Am I right, Colin?"

All eyes turned on Colin in his quiet corner. It was as if he sat under the shade of an umbrella. Julie wondered if he was feeling the same chagrin as she. The two of them had been silent observers at the table, almost a team, pitted against the crescendoing egos of the other two.

Colin sputtered affably into his unruly beard, "Sure, I guess that's an accurate depiction of me. I imagine I can be quite a handful at times."

"And lucky to have me stick by you!"

"And that too." His throat gurgled with its ever-ready chuckle.

Julie rebelled inside. Did he really believe he was lucky to have Sylvia stick by him? Was he really so helpless on his own that he was grateful to Sylvia for propping him up? After only three hours of Sylvia's voice and manner Julie was ready for her guests to leave. But they weren't ready to go yet. William might even need help going. He had heard nothing of Sylvia and Colin's exchange. He sat there in a stupor. Julie could imagine his brain savoring the swirling sensations and delirium of alcohol, for his face appeared lost in the exquisite pleasure of his libido. Suddenly his slithery voice made a fresh entrance, "My birthday is next Saturday."

"Wonderful, congratulations," the others chorused.

He basked in the attention, revealing a missing tooth on the upper right side.

"And being that I'm still one year shy of sixty, I want something really special for my birthday. I'd like to know what you women could give me that would be extra special. I'm all alone after all."

"Why don't we organize a dinner, and each of us can cook one of our favorite dishes for the party," Julie said hastily.

William thought about it before replying, "Yes, I'd like that, a party at my place. Let's have a party."

"You have the perfect place for it," Sylvia said, "with all those frescoed rooms."

His head dropped back to stretch or expose his flaccid neck, "But I want more, this is my birthday after all. I want something that really stands out to mark it. You women should know how to bring this all about. That's your job, your gift."

"Well, William, let's see…," Sylvia said, catching his drift. "What could we do…. I know, we could bring in a giant cake, and when you opened it—"

"No, we wouldn't do that," Julie said.

Sylvia's jack-in-the-box smile burned Julie's face like a gunshot, "No, we wouldn't do that, would we? Ha-ha!"

"But it's my birthday," William whimpered, "and I feel I'm entitled to something really unusual. Come on, I know you women can think up an incredible treat worthy of my special day."

"I don't like where this is heading, William," Sylvia said, schoolmarm to schoolboy.

"Why? Isn't it better to be open and say the things we feel? Why should we hide what we think?"

"I agree, in principle, and I think having a party is a perfectly wonderful idea, let's do it. We can send out an e-mail."

"You didn't answer my question—I asked why should we suppress our deepest feelings? We're all human after all, we all think and feel the same way, so why should one topic of conversation be more acceptable than another?"

"Because that's the way it is when you're with company," Sylvia said. "And why isn't it special enough if all of your friends come over for a party and bring all the food and beverage? I think that's quite an offering."

William didn't hear her. He was too busy scrounging around in his swimming mind, "I was thinking of… what's his name? The American artist, Andrew… Andrew—"

"Wyeth?" Julie suggested.

"No, the other one, Warhol. Andy Warhol. I was just thinking about how Andy Warhol had a birthday party once. I read about it. It was one of those incredibly flashy affairs, packed with all his artsy friends. All of a sudden, this beautiful, sexy young woman came up to him, right in the middle of all the crowded festivities, and pulled down his pants and performed fellatio on him right then and there. Now that's what I consider something really special for a birthday. What a lucky man he was. I can't say I've known that pleasure more than a couple of times myself, but when it's happened it's been something indescribably wonderful, so wonderful that I wouldn't be an honest man if I didn't say I wouldn't mind having more of it, if I could ever be so lucky."

"Well, William, if you're really intent on meeting someone you have to put your mind to it," Sylvia said, as if nothing unusual had been said.

Julie admired her aplomb, for she herself felt paralyzed—and what was Colin thinking? His face revealed nothing. Perhaps, like her, he was wondering when this party was going to end.

Drops of grappa continued to land in William's glass. "I didn't say I was intent on meeting someone, I'm happy the way I am."

"You mean carrying a torch for Gretchen?"

"But I told you I love her. I called her today and I said to her: Do you know that I love you? And by God, do you know where she was when she got my call? At Tiffany's bar looking at diamonds! That's where I'd like to be, at Tiffany's bar." He flashed his missing tooth at them.

No one answered. He was too far gone, repeating himself and unaware of it. Sylvia looked at Colin, "I think we should be heading home, dear, it's late."

Julie hid her relief as she helped the trio into their coats and graciously ushered them to the door, thanking them for their gifts and their company. Sylvia and Colin passed through the arched double doors first, Colin ducking a little. Julie was sure they were happy to breathe the cold night air, like an elixir. When she turned to repeat her goodbyes to William, he paused, as if to start a new conversation that would allow him to take his seat again. He could even finish the bottle of grappa. And perhaps, if left alone together, he might succeed in convincing Julie of his allures. All of that was readable in his unctuous face.

Panic filled her, and she touched his elbow to urge him out the door. He gave slight resistance, but in the end his pedigree won out and he left. Still, Julie didn't trust his departure, even though she heard car doors shutting and engines revving in the driveway. William might return on some excuse, a forgotten item, his scarf or house keys—it seemed sure to happen. Hurriedly, she made the rounds, locking the shutters to all four doors downstairs as if just ahead of her intruder. Her heart was pounding as she raced upstairs and secured the last door in her studio. She was safe now. But she didn't feel safe.

The house was silent, in its hollow, cavernous, necropolis way. It was the Capulet's tomb in *Romeo and Juliet,* where perils lurked. She might have sealed someone in by mistake—he might step out from behind a column at any moment and scare her.

She drew up her shoulders and returned downstairs to clean up. She put on music to make the place feel normal. She moved dishes from the table to the counter and tried to regain her love of solitude and peace. But it was no good—strange sounds could be heard in the driveway. Was it a car? Her heart pounded so hard she no longer breathed. She flew back upstairs to get her cell phone in case she needed to call... but who? She didn't even know the number for 911 in Italy. She saw a missed call on the phone's screen just as the cowbell above her studio door clanged, followed by loud knocking on the sealed shutters. She gasped for breath, blood thundering in her temples, ears, and chest. Terror had completely possessed her. Was William really there? Could he get in? Who could she call?

"Julie!"

"What do you want? Why are you here? This isn't appropriate, you have to leave." The world was surreal—her voice came from the ceiling, not from her own throat.

"Julie!" She heard sentences of munched words, a familiar rhythm of indecipherable language—it was Mario, not William!

But what did he want? Why was he there? Did he think because one man had left her house late at night it was fine for another man to show up? She would have to move! She wasn't safe in the Sabina.

She opened the French door a crack and spoke her basic Italian through the shutter slats. "It's late, you scared me. What's wrong?"

"I came to check on you. I phoned but you didn't answer."

She opened the shutter. They smiled at each other, Julie still afraid.

"I was worried," he said. "A BMW came out of your driveway with a drunk driver—he banged into my wall, and then at the corner, crashed into the dumpster. He sped away."

"I'm so sorry. And thank you for checking. Friends came over for dinner and he got drunk. But I'm fine. All the doors are locked. It's safe here. I'm sorry I didn't hear the phone and you had to come over. "

"*Va bene*, Julie, *buona notte.*"

"Thank you, Mario, thank you so much."

"Boh! You shouldn't be living here all alone."

"I know. We can talk about it tomorrow."

"Get a dog."

"I will, *buona notte, grazie tantissimo.*"

She locked the doors again, but didn't return downstairs to clean up. The only strength she had left was for brushing her teeth and going to bed. It was with relief but not trust that she locked her bedroom door that night and climbed into the bed's icy sheets. Soon daybreak would come.

MUSIC MECCA

From mid-December until early spring, the Sabina gorged on rain, its porous rock like a massive sponge. The dry, baking summer lay ahead, so it was necessary for the olives and underground reservoirs to take in as much water as possible. Most mornings Julie found the mountains steeped in fog, with Soratte and Cosce rising out of the white cloud, their peaks purplish black from the soaking rain. One time it had been the opposite: fog covering just their tops, as if they'd been decapitated. On this February morning, something new and beautiful was happening. Long strands of fog curled through the valleys, which themselves wound through hillocks like emerald green carpets embroidered by nature and accented by dirt roads that looked like wavy stripes.

Sabina winters were nippy because of the mountains and the wind. The Sabinese rarely took off their jackets, mainly because most homes and shops were unheated because of the exorbitant fuel cost. Families relied on their fireplaces when they gathered for meals. Bedrooms were ice cold, sheets were freezing, *gelidi,* and mold grew in the dampest corners. Julie frugally used her household heat. Upstairs in her studio, she ran an electric radiator, but any time she cooked in the kitchen or read on the living-room couch or in bed, the 45-degree air quickly penetrated her bones, making her limbs jerk when she tried to use them. She had broken a few dishes that way. She soon learned to turn on the central heat a few times a day to keep the thick stone walls warm—otherwise they took three days to warm up again. When friends came for lunch, tea, or dinner, she turned on the heat, as others did when she visited them. Heat was part of hospitality.

In the cold and wet months of January and February, the farmers, the *contadini,* pruned their olive trees and burned the branches, too often clouding the panorama and clear air with suffocating smoke. But it was useless to propose an ecological alternative, such as a mulching machine, for with a growl the farmers would wave it off, not even interested in listening. Burning was tradition, but more important, it was free. The Sabanese farmers obdurately followed an ancient way of life: the hand-wrought cultivation of food. It was an art. Bent and broken, swollen and disabled by their mid-sixties, they deserved special honor.

Julie was pondering the hardship and glory of the *contadini* while waiting for her college friend, Jason Talbert, to wake up. Already his winter break from teaching art in New York City was nearing its end, and they'd hardly begun to see all the things she had wanted to show him in the Sabina and Rome. He had brought along his adorable bulldog Daisy, who was now sleeping almost in the arms of Orso, Julie's adopted sheepdog whose elderly owner in the valley had died.

Jason's footsteps began their slow, thumping descent on the living-room staircase. "*Buon giorno, bellina,*" he called out sonorously. "Sorry I overslept again, culpa mia."

"*Sono qui, nella cucina,*" Julie called back, "*con i bravissimi cani.*"

He came into the room, tall, dark-haired, and boyish. His smile was quick to flash and happy, and his brown eyes with big whites rolled around expressively. He loved food, and his shape was bearish and huggable.

"My God, look at the fog today!" he said and immediately stepped outside to inhale the atmosphere as if his deep suctions could satisfy his eyesight. "Brrrr!" he laughed, scampering back indoors.

"Bare feet don't help."

"But I want to feel every bit of this Sabina experience," Jason said, "especially since I have only two days left. How can that be? Where did the time go?" He swooped up tap-dancing Daisy and snuggled her head. "Well, good morning to you too, my little darling! Has Orso been taking good care of you?"

"Help yourself to breakfast and then let's hit the road."

"Aye-aye, signora, but can't I get my cappuccino at the Antico Caffè?

"Of course."

"Good-morning to you, too, Orso, you didn't have to get up for me, but since you did, how about a piece of my toast, as soon as I make it?"

That morning, under threatening clouds the old friends drove several kilometers with the dogs to the communal pastures called *prati*. For centuries these undulating meadows between craggy mountains had served as town grazing land. Near the meadows' entrance, abandoned stone buildings clustered on a hillside and were now inhabited by pigs. Along the miles of dirt roads that looped through the pastures, white cows and dark horses—all tagged or branded—lazily passed the days. Long ago, townspeople had come to this cooler spot in summertime. But it was all ruins now and only the imagination could fill in children frolicking in the fields while their mothers washed and cooked outdoors. Presumably the men had remained on the farms to cut and bale hay, tend gardens, and care for the olive and fruit trees. Annual festivals and picnics still took place here, and on Sundays many nature lovers walked the trails.

"This is wonderful!" Jason said. "I love it! Not just the pastures—but the ruins. Why do we love ruins so much?"

"Because they conjure up the past," Julie said.

"Yes, and it was so romantic."

"Except for all the killing and inhumanity."

"True. You spoiled my vision."

"Ruins deepen my sense of existence."

"They make mine seem more ephemeral than ever."

"It's the same thing. I wonder how Italians feel about them, having lived among them for hundreds of years."

"Just old hat. We'll have to take a poll."

"Yeah, it would depend who you asked. The farmers and the aristocrats would have different perspectives."

"It's too complicated—leave it for the sociologists. For us, the answer is enjoy for yourself, or with a friend."

Orso, a dog with authority around other animals, began barking ferociously and then galloped off toward a herd of pink piglets on the other side of a shallow stream with an earthen bridge. The piglets squealed and trotted away from the bridge as fast as their stubby legs would go. Daisy timidly followed Orso's lead, and now, side by side they blocked access to the bridge, creating mayhem among the piglets as they tried to figure out which way to go to reach their hillside shelters.

Suddenly loud bellows sounded from the ruins and several enormous, muddy pigs charged down the hill on their own stumpy legs. Daisy yelped in fear, began to run back to Jason, but at the same time felt torn to play a role in Orso's game, and eventually tiptoed back to him. As the furious mama and papa pigs dashed through the stream and closed in on the dogs, Orso backed off a bit, barking at them. Then, out of dog pride he once again feigned aggression toward the piglets, which squealed in panic, but a few decibels lower, now that their elders were present. The big pigs covered the little pigs' rear flank, and together they all scuttled through the streambed, escaping to the other side. One humongous pig stayed behind to threaten Orso, while the rest trotted speedily up the hill to the shelters. With a few disgusted grunts, the pig patriarch turned away and headed home. Orso answered with outraged barking but did not pursue his adversary.

"Come here, Daisy, come here sweetheart, what did you think of all those pigs? Was that exciting? What do you think of this Sabina-land? Would you want to live here? Shall we move?"

"Nooo, I like New York City, it feels much safer. But coming for visits to see Orso and Julie will be fine," Daisy answered primly through Jason's voice. "And with a little practice, maybe I can take on the piglets all by myself!"

Jason grinned at Julie, "Don't mind me."

"I won't. Orso talks too."

"Go figure."

Further along the old road a natural phenomenon awaited them. It was a stand of bare winter trees covering a hill. They were a single species planted long ago after deforestation. Now, in the faint sunlight filtering through clouds, the trunks and filigree branches lit up with an extraterrestrial phosphorescence, which was the lichen covering their bark.

"Wow. That is amazing," Jason said, staring at the glowing forest. "That does it. I'm moving here. Daisy, you'll just have to adapt."

"Do you think you could really live here?" Julie said.

"Easily. But I'd have to learn the language. And support myself."

"Two simple hurdles."

"What's your secret?"

"The sale of our house. It can keep me going a few more years and then I'll have to get serious—and I'll be pushing sixty. A perfect age to go job hunting," she grinned. "Though I'm also looking for opportunities here."

"Maybe you can sell your Sabina paintings."

"Ha, I've already been through that, don't you remember our idealistic days of youth?"

"Hey, I'm still counting on it. When I'm ninety they're going to be writing about me as the next Picasso. So, what're you going to do to stay here? And come on, let's be realistic. What about Italian hospitals? Are you really going to die here alone with one or two friends checking in on you now and then and by that stage only out of determined duty?"

"Don't be so practical." But his words expressed thoughts she herself occasionally considered.

"Come on, Julie, what about Annie?"

"She's fine, enjoying her career, and planning to visit me in June."

"But in the long run, when she's married with kids and you're too decrepit to harvest olives anymore...."

"I can't think that far, Jason. I just got here. I'm still in the daze of discovery and wonder. I love it here, as if my true nature found its true home. And I'm making friends slowly—maybe not what would be my best matches in an ideal world, but there's community here, and for me it's even more fulfilling."

"Wow, I'd better think more seriously about a sabbatical, to enjoy this splendor together."

"I wish you would."

Since college nothing had altered their friendship. They got up each day seeking the same satisfactions from life—art and architecture, nature and exercise, and pursuit of the arts. Attraction had never been an issue because Jason was gay. And although Julie had shared his elation when falling in love, or his broken-heart when a relationship failed, she had nothing to do with his social life and knew few of his friends. Together they shared a private world of their own.

"I've got it!" Jason said with sudden inspiration. "I'll join Music Mecca and do my art while supported by the community."

"I thought you said Music Mecca wanted musicians? And how did you get hooked up with these people in the first place?"

"Elsa, from our Painting-II class."

"I don't remember her."

"Well, she's still around and still painting—she actually found a commercial niche and sells from her website. Anyhow, last year she had an artist's residency in Boulder and sublet her apartment to a dancer named Tammy. When I told Elsa I was coming to visit you, she said Tammy and her fiancé were starting an artists' colony in the Sabina. So I emailed Tammy, and that's how we got invited for dinner."

The dinner was the following night at Music Mecca's sixteenth-century abbey. "They plan to grow their own food," Jason added.

"I want to explore the abbey," Julie said.

"I want to live in it. Too bad I'm about to leave."

"It can be your reconnaissance visit for your future."

"*Perfetto!*"

The next day, they drove to Greccio and visited St. Francis's sanctuary. He had created several sanctuaries in the area, and in summertime, pilgrims walked between them on peaceful trails imbued with the saint's spirit of goodness. The Greccio sanctuary was the oldest and dated to 1217. It was famous for being the site of the first nativity scene, created by St. Francis himself. A newer church from the 1960s stood adjacent to the original chapel and displayed hundreds of nativity scenes by folk artists from around the world, most of the creations kitsch, but at the same time touching for the obvious love and labor that had gone into their making.

Julie and Jason concentrated the ancient dwelling. From its entrance with a simple altar, a cave threaded back to St. Francis's personal retreat. There, behind Plexiglas was the worn rock where the saint had slept. The white surface reclined and curved badly, but it was possible to imagine a thin, robed body twisting to fit the slab. The back of the cave— barely a crawl space—enclosed the bed. Julie imagined the total darkness at night when St. Francis snuffed out his oil lamp. She stood transfixed by the reality of sleeping in that black catacomb surrounded by nocturnal insects and critters. The image imprinted on her brain with claustrophobic horror.

Luckily they ate lunch on the wide open piazza of rather shabby Greccio, a few kilometers from the sanctuary. Bundled up for the cool temperature, they ate *pasta con funghi* from a rickety cafe table—the only place open—while drab locals ate inside and watched them through a dirty picture window.

"I never realized how lucky I am to have a bed," Jason said.

"I couldn't take total enclosure like that," Julie said. "I have to see stars or even a black sky."

"But in those days if you were poor and didn't have a workforce at your disposal, you looked for a cave to get your start," Jason said.

"In a few more centuries, people will be pitying us for this lunch."

"But they won't know what they missed," Jason said, popping a forkful of pasta into his mouth and making a rapt face. "Mmm."

"Julie nodded. "You wouldn't have thought good food could come out of that hole-in-the-wall."

"I guess grandma is in the kitchen."

"And here comes her daughter-in-law."

A thin, stooped woman of indeterminate middle age, her face badly worn from smoking, came out in her faded print dress and flapping slippers to remove their plates, which bread had wiped spotless.

"*Buono?*" she rasped.

"*Buonissimo.*"

"*Stupendo,*" Jason said.

She smiled, having known the answer before she asked. "Caffè?"

"*Si, due,*" Julie answered. The frail figure, now coughing, scurried back indoors with their dishes.

"Did you remember to bring your pictures?" Jason asked.

"Yes." Julie retrieved the pack from her bag and passed them to Jason. His head bent studiously over each frame while she described her first olive harvest back in November.

"Who's the hunk without his shirt?"

"Sergio, my occasional helper. His girlfriend's pregnant but they're in no hurry to get married. He lives with his parents and she lives with hers. They spend the weekends together."

"What happens when the baby comes?"

"They haven't decided yet."

"How did you meet him?"

"Mario. Mario organized my harvest. He even took me to the supply store for nets and cases, so I'd get the local price and not the foreigners' rate."

"No price tags in Italy."

"Not everywhere. And for special customers there are discounts."

"So these nets catch all the olives."

"And the little rakes pull them down into the net. See how Sergio and I are holding up the ends of the net? We're about to shake the olives down to the other end where they get poured into a case."

"How many cases do you get from one tree?"

"It depends—my little trees don't fill a case, but the big tree by the kitchen fills three."

"I want to come back next year for the harvest."

"Maybe you'll join Music Mecca for a sabbatical."

They drove home over mountain roads in late afternoon, their eyes taking in bleak rural scenery where hardship for families still existed, as their dreary, white-washed cottages with survival implements strewn about the yard showed. Rain began to fall as they drew closer to their own constellation of more prosperous hill-towns. Their thoughts turned to the evening ahead and the salad they had signed up to contribute to the dinner at Music Mecca.

But once home, they went to their rooms to check their email and enjoy some quiet time. Around six they reconvened in the kitchen to prepare their dish. Working side-by-side and being artists, they couldn't help but concoct masterpieces: two wide pasta bowls filled with freshly washed lettuces, endive, radicchio, and *riccioli* (escarole), the various leaves mixing their shapes, textures, and colors. On top, as an enticing decoration they had added sections of grated carrots, cherry tomatoes, red pepper strips, cucumber slices, pear triangles, and red onion. In the center they arranged small chunks of aged blue cheese topped with toasted walnuts. Finished, they stood back and admired their tantalizing creations.

"Can't we eat mini salads right now?" Jason asked, snitching a lump of cheese from his bowl and popping it into his mouth.

"No, we have to starve for this feast, especially after a pasta lunch."

"You're right, but you're too rigid. I read that too much self-discipline makes you tired," Jason said.

"That explains why sometimes I just want to deflate all the way," Julie said. "You know, like the Wicked Witch of the West melting through the floorboards."

"Ha! Those ghostly Sabina spirits are getting to you."

"There aren't any ghosts."

"This house is spooky at night!"

"The mountain breathes, that's all. Stop eating all the cheese." She crumbled more cheese over his salad.

"That's why I have this eternal paunch, no matter how much I exercise," he said, squeezing his tummy. "Maybe if I join Music Mecca I won't eat so much. Knowing that I had to hoe, grow, and pick every green bean I ate might make me less hungry all the time."

"You like food. You're human. You're in deep middle age. It's normal to carry a few extra pounds. Besides, you look fantastic."

"Grazie, Julia, for permission to self-indulge one last time." He popped the largest chunk of cheese into his mouth and beat a retreat from the bowls.

It was a pitch-black night without moon or stars when they set out for Music Mecca. The winding roads were a challenge to drive, especially with the wipers slapping back and forth, for the rain had not abated. As they wound through the mountains westward, they passed several shadowy castle ruins on hilltops, their jagged towers still imposing like the dukes and bishops who had once ruled them.

"I want to explore these places next time I come," Jason said. "I've fallen in love with this place. I'm really serious about joining Music Mecca. But I'd have to convince them to take a painter instead of a fiddler."

"Maybe it would work, and just think—an old abbey—plenty of space and amazing antiquity."

"I'd run the mess hall. For life. And I'd like it to be old-fashioned. Huge wooden cupboards with big keyholes for locking, and I'd wear the keys jangling from my hip. No sneaking any of my quince jam!"

"It would be an austere life, no frills, frigid winters."

"Would I have to sleep on a rock like St. Francis?"

"No. Music Mecca would let you buy an Ikea bed—spartan but comfortable."

"Deal!"

He began to hum with his visions of living at Music Mecca, and Julie began to wonder what it would be like to have him thirty minutes away at the abbey. They'd take weekend jaunts to Naples and other archaeological sites. Of course he might meet someone at Music Mecca and do all his explorations with the new companion. But still, on occasion, they'd take excursions together and in summer paint landscapes en plein air.

At the foot of a twinkling Umbrian hilltown, they turned off the main road and followed a potholed lane further down the incline into an immense valley, where they came to the broken

gates of the decaying abbey. It was completely dark and shut-
tered—abandoned—except for a single bulb over a primitive door
at one corner of the building, the old service entrance. Lumpy
overgrown land lay all around; it would be a challenge to restore
and cultivate. Shadowy, scrawny cypresses stood like sentries along
the narrow driveway that led to the abbey's courtyard. They drove
in bumping hard over the rutted dirt and parked close to the lit
door. Julie waited for a minute before turning off the headlights, so
that they could peer at the abbey through darkness and rain. It was
a long, two-storied building of yellow tufa stone, with a simple
church at the far end. The monks had not lived in luxury, nor had
they lacked basic comfort—shelter and hearth.

"My God," Jason breathed, "it's even got a campanile! I'm
definitely buying in. It hasn't been touched, it's ready to bring
back to life."

"Are you really ready to restore fifty-thousand square meters
with your bare hands, one rock at a time, followed by plastering,
painting, plumbing, wiring, roofing—all to EU standards?"

"But I'd have helpers."

"The musicians would exploit your artistic training and talent."

"I could do a Sistine Chapel for them! That would be my
contribution—twenty years painting original frescoes from scaffolding. And I'd also volunteer to serve as art director—maybe
twelve hours a week at a desk telling all the laborers what to do."

Julie laughed, "Okay, we'd better get in there with our salads
and get you signed up. Are you ready to make a run for it?"

"Ready."

They got out fast, opened the back doors, whisked out the
salads and wine bottle, and loped over the lumpy, soaked ground
to the lit door that leaked wintry air through its rotted frame.
No one inside heard their repeated knocking, but Julie and Jason
could hear loud music hammering the abbey's thick stone walls,
walls that had never heard such pagan sounds. Julie saw a pile of

firewood next to the door. She grabbed a wet log and pounded the door with it. Within seconds they were greeted and ushered in out of the rain. They passed through a cold, dank vestibule into a large kitchen heated by a good fire. Jazz was playing loudly.

Six bodies swarmed around them to exchange greetings, take their coats, and exclaim thanks for their offerings. Randy Meister, Tammy's fiancé and the founder of Music Mecca, stared through the Cellophane at the salad he had taken from Julie. "Oooh, look at this, everyone. A baroque sculpture. What? You brought two of them? Let's put one on the table for now; I doubt we'll need the other." He took command of both salads, planting one on the large, square dinner table and securing the other behind a dense fence of bottles and jars on the counter. Julie glanced at Jason to see if he had noticed Randy's confiscation of the second salad, but Jason's happy face focused on an animated conversation with Hans.

Randy took charge of drinks, or "aperitifs," as he called them. He was tall and burly, his chest a solid block that got in his way. He was a singer, and that organ-grinder's box under his shoulders held his wind. Yet his movements around the room were agile, like a dancer doing leaps, which his lizard pants emphasized. He had badly cut brown hair streaked with red henna, and an artiste's facial hair outlined his mouth and jaw. The lips cut a quarter-moon straight down, following the mustache lines that connected to his jaw-trimmings. His features, though regular, appeared puffy, as early middle age or poor lifestyle took their toll. Mod rectangular glasses concealed his eyes, their expression, but something about them came through the lenses as reddish, lashless, and calculating. His energy was palpable, not just from his deft movements around the room, but also from the alacrity of his voice and authoritarian delivery.

"Julie, what aperitif would you like?"

"Hmm, I think I'll wait and have wine with dinner."

"But we have everything here, including interesting nonalcoholic drinks." His right arm swept the well-stocked bar on the counter. "For instance, I could make you a yummy drink with hazelnut syrup."

"That sounds good, I'll try it."

When he presented her with the milky glass, he said, "It would be better with club soda, but here we have to settle for their bubbly water."

She sipped. "It's delicious, thank you."

And he was off to mix more drinks.

The stark room, lit by a few bare bulbs on the walls, was Music Mecca's temporary headquarters, with a shabby couch and chairs in front of the fireplace, the large table near the kitchen counter, and tall cabinets along one wall for storage. The cabinet doors had been covered with pieces of paper telling the team what to do toward executing their mission. The team included the principals, Randy and Tammy, their friend Brian, who served as chief of staff, and three part-timers: Hans, their German business-plan developer; Chiara, a pretty Italian graduate student in philosophy; and Susan, a Canadian flute player living with her Italian boyfriend in Rome. These three didn't live at the abbey, though they came for several days at a time to volunteer for the community. Hans came less often because he lived in Germany.

Julie went over to Tammy to get better acquainted. Dressed in a bulky sweater and black baseball cap, Tammy looked like a college cheerleader, though she was probably in her mid-thirties. Her pert, attractive face showed mostly her full smile and good teeth, for the baseball cap shaded her eyes. Little by little Julie made out the red script above the visor: Music Mecca. When Tammy talked, her inner exuberance couldn't be contained. She lunged forward, tilted back, and vigorously circled her head. Her happy, vociferous voice broke into a ready laugh every few sentences, and then the laugh morphed into a silent, head-nodding guffaw, with front teeth protruding deliberately, like a cartoon character.

It seemed appropriate to talk about her black cat, Molly, sitting like a porcelain figure on the chair next to them, which faced the table, where a plate of ostrich prosciutto and pecorino cheese had been set out for nibbling. Every now and then Molly's head stretched forward from her neck with a paw lifting involuntarily. "Ah, ah, ah," Tammy warned, and the cat's paw drew back.

"I'm sure Molly's going to be just fine here," Tammy said. "She's already settled in and today began scratching at the door. She's ready to explore the big wide world out there, aren't ya, cutie pie?" She bent to nuzzle the cat's head.

"Do you know about the dumpster culture for cats?" Julie asked with a twinkle in her eye.

"No, what happens at the dumpster?"

"All the cats hang out there at night; it's their pub. Even the well-groomed house cats show up and mix in with the scruffy ones."

"Oh… I think I'll keep Molly in at night. I'm sure we can give her enough *indoor* party life, isn't that right, Miss Mollykins? You love parties, don't you?" She again nuzzled the cat with her cheek and lips, "You're our voodoo queen, aren't you?"

Julie circulated, hoping to meet everyone before the dinner. Jason waved her over and introduced Hans. "He wants to visit the *prati* and see the pigs and the illuminated forest."

"That's right, if you have time during my next visit from Germany, I'd like to come over and see this place. I'm a walker, in the same category as your John Muir," he smiled with friendly eyes. "This past summer, I walked from Austria to Slovakia and then on to Prague."

"Amazing—how long did that take?"

"The whole summer, but I made stops along the way. That's part of the fun of it—meeting people."

"We have tons of trails here. Some were old roads to major cities—rocky mule paths."

"Yes, I've been collecting maps of the area for Music Mecca," Hans said and drew them over to a topographical map taped to the wall. "Here's the abbey." He pointed to a black circle amid the wavy lines of the Sabina's mountainous terrain.

"And here's Monte Donato," Jason said, having already studied the map with Hans. "Julie's domain."

"You'll have to cross a lot of gorges to walk there from here," Julie said just as her eye caught a colorful image on the table below the map. It was a tarot card of the emperor figure propped up on a miniature easel. Crowned, cloaked in royal red, the sovereign filled his throne powerfully, his right hand holding a staff that symbolized his ability to enforce his will.

"Look at this," Julie said, reaching for the card.

But just then Randy's hand swept in, pushing back the easel, "Yes, in some of my festival work, I've recreated the ancient rites of tarot."

"What are those?" Julie asked.

"I'll tell you in a minute. Brian, is that grill just about ready?" Randy called across the room rather testily. "We've got to get this show on the road, or we're going to be eating at midnight." He waited for an answer to come through the half-open door but none came. "Need some help?" he said, barely containing his irritation. After two more beats he excused himself and exited out the door to where Brian tended the grill. Julie wondered how Randy treated Brian during their everyday interactions.

Julie asked Hans where the bathroom was and he pointed to a door across the room, "Just follow the corridor back and it's on the left—and very cold, sorry!"

Julie slipped out. Someone had put a nightlight into a socket to light the way. The hallway was frigid, unheated, but now she was inside the abbey and rooms led off the corridor. She wanted to see them and opened the first door on her right. There was no light switch and the shutters to the solitary window were closed. It was a small room and a knapsack was on a cot.

She continued down the hallway, figuring that the other doors would reveal similar cells for the former monks. The bathroom door was open with another nightlight inside. The facility was basic and heavily utilized with everyone's toiletries on a dilapidated table. The porcelain tub was an old model, half-size with a seat, and had a spray nozzle for washing. Julie gingerly opened another door in the bathroom to see where it led. She stepped into a chamber a bit musty from mold growing on the old plaster walls. The faint bathroom light was enough to reveal the furnishings—cushion-covered mattresses on the carpeted floor, straight from European paintings of sultans' harems. Julie could see Tammy's creamy flesh stretched there among the velvets and satins, her face laughing with invitation, for she was her chieftain's favorite siesta dessert, at least at this time, for competition had already moved in. Then there was the throne, also surrounded by luxurious cushions. The wood-carved frame was of such imperious stature that the pope himself might have owned it in Castel Sant'Angelo in the 1500s. But somehow, one of his bishops had squirreled it away for his own aggrandizement at his Sabina fiefdom. Probably Randy had found it in some secret place in the abbey, for it wasn't an item to be left behind when the abbey closed for good in the 1960s. Her eye alighted upon an old leather suitcase amid the erotic appurtenances. The playthings, she thought, and was about to step over and open it when the shadow of a vulture cast over her path and she swung around with a scream to find Randy.

"What are you doing here?"

"I had to go to the bathroom."

"This is the bathroom," his straight arm pointed the direction and told her to march.

"The door was open," she mumbled. "Sorry, I didn't mean to intrude."

"I'll see you back in the kitchen. We're ready to eat."

When she got back to the kitchen, Randy was instructing everyone where to sit at the big square table. Chairs were scraping.

"Hey Tammy, what about some candles? We need a little atmosphere in here. Obviously the previous dwellers wanted just the opposite," Randy said.

"Coming right up," Tammy chortled.

Eventually they were all seated with the candles lit and the center of the table laden with serving bowls of steaming pumpkin risotto. Randy and Tammy sat opposite Julie and Susan. Silence naturally descended and all eyes lifted to Randy, their host and leader.

"What do you say we begin this feast with a little vesper, just to synchronize our digestive powers?" Randy said affably, but the look he gave each of them as his eye circled the table was stern.

Agreeable murmurs came from the Music Mecca group, with a more audible "Good idea, hon!" from Tammy.

Randy's eyes, through the opacity of his glasses, bore into Julie, "As you probably know I'm very interested in Gregorian chants, ancient Italian music and instruments, and community spirituality, something we've lost sight of in the States, if we ever had it. You and Jason can sit back and enjoy our little ditty, or hum along, suit yourselves. Hey, and what about doing away with the lights, Tammy? Will candles be good enough for everybody?"

Tammy jumped up and snapped off the bare bulbs, plunging the room into darkness, which then adjusted to the flickering candlelight on the table.

"Is this all right?" Randy repeated. Consent murmured happily.

"*Much* better," Tammy laughed.

Randy tapped his wine glass three times with his knife. "This is a seventh-century compline, or end-of-the-day hymn, which I've translated from Latin." His sonorous voice then filled every corner of the room with musical beauty. The verses didn't matter, Julie thought, it was the sound that counted, and Randy's voice had divine endowment. She couldn't reconcile the unpleasant man with the pure and saintly voice that flowed effortlessly out of him. When he finished singing, he flashed a grin around the table as if to say, Yes, that is why I'm in charge here. He picked up his fork, "Dig in!"

It was already nine-thirty, and the famished diners inhaled the risotto while forking it rhythmically into their mouths, the aroma doubling their intake. Randy soon lifted his glass and reminded everyone that Susan was responsible for their culinary ecstasy. Susan, with a scarf wrapped several turns around her neck to treat her sore throat, answered in a squeaky voice, as if strangling, "I thought risotto would be a good change from pasta." Then everyone discussed how to make risotto. Soon, conversation broke down into smaller groups, Julie learning more about Susan's three years in Rome living with her Italian boyfriend. "But now he's gone to London for a year to learn English, and if Music Mecca hadn't come up as an opportunity for me, I would have gone with him. But I don't want to leave now, and I know we can make it through one year with a long-distance relationship."

"You can take those cheap airlines to see each other—one cent for the flight and thirty-nine euros for tax."

"Exactly. He'll come home a few times and I'll go there a few times, and *basta*, the year will be over before we know it."

"What kinds of things are you doing with Music Mecca?"

"Ever since moving to Rome, I've gotten further and further away from my flute music, partly out of necessity. I'm not thrilled with my current job—it's with an NGO. Here, with Music Mecca, I'll be able to give performances again and fulfill my creative side. And I'll also help organize festivals. Randy's really good at transformative art. He takes old music and rituals and creates new contexts for them. We put on a festival here last summer and that's why the town is giving us the abbey. They saw how our music event brought everyone together. Music's always been a tradition for strengthening communities, but nowadays, people don't connect any more—we don't have time. Music naturally creates bonds, shared joy, and a lot of people feel genuine love when they participate in music festivals."

"It sounds great," Julie said. "Like a love-in."

"Our festivals are on a much higher level than a love-in," Randy shot across the table. "We're working with the mayor and the local church to make this town the region's center of music and cultural activity. Who wants more risotto besides me?" He pushed back his chair and went for the pot on the stove. Hans and Jason welcomed another scoop, and Randy scraped the last tasty goo into his bowl. "Fini! Exceptional work, Susan."

"Thank you."

He put the pot in the sink and then came to stand by Julie, "I think we'll have your salad next, would that be all right?"

"Of course." Julie got up to toss the salad with the balsamic vinaigrette they had brought.

"And the grilled meat will be along in just a few minutes," he added, returning to his seat. "Do you want to check on it, Brian?"

Brian got right up to check the grill. He was a quiet, gentle person, offering help but keeping to the background. He had shaved his head in the style of many Italian men who were balding and he actually looked Italian, including his medium-height and muscular build.

Julie had just finished tossing the salad when Brian returned to say he wasn't sure if the meat was done. Randy jumped up to check it, telling Brian to serve the salad on clean plates.

Brian brought a stack of plates to the table and began doling out the salad, with the red pepper, radicchio, and tomato shining in their coating of vinaigrette. It was clear he was going to run out of salad before everyone was served. "I'll toss the other one," Julie said getting up.

"It won't go to waste," Susan said. "I love salad."

"I love salad too," Chiara smiled. Her heart-shaped face was beautiful in the candlelight. Dark tresses rippled past her shoulders, enhancing the virginal sensuality that radiated from her dark eyes, eyebrows, rich red lips, and soft complexion. She would be a perfect model for Leonardo da Vinci, Julie thought, and then wondered if she herself might invite Chiara over to sit for a portrait.

Brian filled his and Hans's plate from the new salad.

"What? Did you open the second salad?" Randy said, returning from the grill and standing over Brian like a comandante.

"There wasn't enough for the last two plates," Julie said.

"And now we can all have seconds," Chiara smiled.

Randy moved away. He didn't like it that the troops had gone against his decision to put away the second salad. He rummaged around the bottles on the counter seeking the right choice for refills.

At the same time, Brian began munching his salad and for a split second lifted his inscrutable eyes to Julie's and breathed, "Thank you," two words nobody else heard.

Julie couldn't help but remember her college days in the early seventies when young men with shaved heads and orange robes hopped barefoot in Washington Square chanting, "Hari Krishna." News articles described distraught parents trying to rescue their sons who had lost their way and joined the community. There was something of the lost, ultra-vulnerable soul in Brian.

Randy returned to the table with a second carafe of red wine.

"*Honey,* shouldn't we put out Julie and Jason's wine?" Tammy asked getting up.

"No need, we can drink up this good stuff first," he said, plunking down the local red as if it were a pitcher of beer.

But Tammy was already putting the bottle of merlot on the table before he finished speaking.

"And don't worry, *honey,* we're going to drink all of this tonight," Randy said, his hand on the carafe's neck. "Anyone ready?"

Julie never saw who uncorked the merlot bottle, but the next time she looked it was open and she helped herself to a glass when Randy wasn't looking. She didn't want a second glass of his rotgut red. The next time she looked, the bottle was empty, as others sneaked refills into their own glasses. Probably Hans had nonchalantly opened the wine. As the volunteer business manager he had nothing to fear from Randy. Meanwhile, Randy had disappeared to tend the grill and soon returned with a platter of jiggling, smelly meat.

His eyes bore through his lenses at Julie, "I hope everyone likes liver, and if they don't, it's not a problem, we won't be offended." He handed her the platter.

"I'm a vegetarian," Hans said, "but it's not a problem, I'm used to this."

"I'm a liver eater," Jason said. "But I never cook it because my kitchen's too small and the smell lasts for days, maybe years."

Julie took a sliver to her plate and passed the platter. She was not a liver eater.

Back in his chair, Randy watched as the platter made its rounds, noting who was and who wasn't a liver eater. When the dish came to its final resting place at his plate, he paused without serving himself, and then, got back up to come to Julie's side, where he took the salad bowl from the table. "I don't think we'll be needing this anymore," he said, looking down at her with the piercing arrows of his vibes.

She smiled innocently wondering what the hell his problem was with the salad.

Seated once again, Randy heaped wiggly liver slices onto his plate and thoroughly enjoyed eating this course of the meal. Tammy told stories at his side, of their tumultuous arrival the month before, but their subsequent integration with the local folks due to her solo dance performance on the town square for Carnevale. "Now everybody knows me, they all wave at me on the street, 'Ciao, Tammy!' It makes getting things done so much easier! I don't have to worry about my bad Italian!" She laughed and then did her nodding, silent guffaw with buck teeth.

"What kind of dance do you do?" Jason asked. "Modern?"

"Oooh, Randolph calls it eclectic, because I borrow from all kinds of traditions, including African and aboriginal cultures. But through Randolph, I've been learning a lot about medieval and Renaissance dance. I throw it all into the mix," she said, a notion that set off her laugh.

"One of the things we plan to do at Music Mecca," Randy said, running his hand over his sated stomach that looked like a continuation of the music box in his chest, "is to research and perform ritual dances, recreating authentic costumes and props. I also have a strong background in experimental ritual theater. I write and direct. I founded several projects that toured Europe and the States, besides creating countless syncretic productions all over the world."

"Well, you're in the right country for festivals involving historic costumes and reenactments," Julie said.

"I wouldn't call what we're doing reenactments," Randy said.

"Oh, sorry, what's the right term?"

"I like to say reconstructions. We're aiming for ritual reconstructions. For instance, if we're doing a concert of early Italian music, we bring it to life by reconstructing its original liturgical context. We're also into synchronicity and how being open to its potential cultivates the spirituality and unity of a community. We're all part of the same energy and dynamism, not to mention love. And by the way, our work isn't limited to Italy. We're talking the world."

Ah, Napoleon! Julie thought, and dismissed him once and for all.

"So, how are you going to find your residents?" Jason asked.

It was obvious from his neutral tone he was no longer an aspiring applicant. "Will you send notices to university music departments for applicants?"

Randy shook his head, "We don't have to recruit—musicians are going to be knocking down the doors to get in with us. We're going to have to carefully select who gets to come here—they have to be able to get along in a communal environment, want what we want," Randy said.

"Yeah, and hoe the garden for dinner," Tammy laughed.

"We'll be sharing everything, like a family."

"Sounds cool," Jason said.

And who will be head of household? Julie thought. Aloud she said, "How long will it take to repair the abbey?"

Tammy and Randy rolled their eyes in unison, "Forever!"

"Right now our sole focus is fundraising," Randy said, waving an arm at the sheets of paper scotch-taped to the cabinets behind him.

"What if you can't raise the money?"

He shrugged, "Then we move somewhere else."

"But we know there's lots of people like us who want this kind of life," Susan said, rewrapping the scarf around her neck.

"We'd be a lot better off without this oboe," Randy said, getting up and turning down the music. "Oboes should be banned from jazz."

"Are oboes in jazz bands?" Julie asked.

"Never! Just on this recording. But I *do* I respect oboists. The oboe is really hard to play, it's a hard art."

"A hard art?" Jason said.

"Randolph has a whole theory on this," Tammy giggled.

"That's right. Just as you have hard and soft sciences, so you have hard and soft arts."

"What's a soft art?" Julie asked.

"The definition of a soft art is any art you can do really badly and still get paid for it," he said.

"Like what?" Jason asked.

"Like acting and directing, those are soft arts. What do those guys do? Nuttin'! And they get paid to do nothing."

"I've seen plenty of films that blew my mind away because of the director's talent, or the actor's," Julie said.

"Sure, I'm not denying there can be great directors and actors—I've directed and acted myself—but there are hordes of pretenders out there doing absolutely nothing. Painting's a medium art," he mumbled as an afterthought, with a little spit to his lips.

Jason and Julie took this in without flinching or even exchanging a look. Their forks kept busy, their smiles stayed in place.

"I think it's time to play the Toast Game," Randy said, setting off giggles in Tammy.

"What's the Toast Game?" Chiara asked skeptically.

"I think you invented it, didn't you, honey?" Tammy said.

"I think I probably did. We go around the room and each person gives a toast."

"I don't want to play this," Chiara said, frowning.

"But you have to," Julie grinned at her.

"That's right," Randy said, adding wine from the carafe to Chiara's glass. "But it's not hard, you'll do fine, sweetie."

"It's a soft art," Jason said.

"Here are the rules: The first person gives a one-line toast, and the next person has to use one word from the toast in his or her toast, and so on, around the room. You can start, Chiara."

"Meee? Not me!"

"The first person has it the easiest, you don't have to think of using another person's word," Randy said.

So she lifted her glass obediently and uttered a few words that no one heard except for Randy, who had to go second. He pondered briefly and then said his line, cleverly morphing Chiara's word "convene" into "convention."

"You changed the word!" Tammy cried out.

"The root's the same, makes the game more interesting."

As each person said their meaningless one-liner, Randy let a pause sink in and then commented, like a critic. Julie took Brian's word "perfection" and wished everyone "perfection of their dreams." After the mandatory pause Randy said, "I guess by perfection you mean attainment."

"Yes," Julie smiled.

As Susan gave the last toast, Julie and Jason exchanged a look that conveyed a mutual desire to leave.

"Hey, I hate to be the party-pooper, but my plane leaves at noon tomorrow, which means catching the 7:40 train to the airport," Jason said.

"We'd better get you home," Julie said. "This has been a wonderful evening and thanks to all of you for having us and for sharing such a delicious meal."

"It was our pleasure," Randy said.

"Your salad was the highlight," Chiara said.

They all got up from the table to say their goodbyes. At the counter, Julie put the leftover salad in a container for Randy for his midnight snack. Brian produced coats and with final reiterations of thanks, Julie and Jason made their escape. Outside they rushed over the lumpy grass to the car and threw themselves in. Julie started the engine and backed out much too fast over the potholes to the main road. The rain had stopped. The countryside was pitch black and silent, asleep until morning. At the corner dumpster three scruffy cats stared at them from the glistening rim.

"I am so glad to get out of there," Julie laughed.

"Me too!" Jason said. "What was his thing about the salad?"

"I have no idea. I think he wanted to save one of them for himself."

"Yeah, that was it—there was a certain greed to him."

"And lasciviousness. He's a cult leader," Julie said.

"I won't be joining Jim Jones to live in the Sabina for the rest of my life, or until I'm told to drink cyanide-laced Kool-Aid."

"But I liked all his disciples."

"Me too, especially Hans. I want to walk the Russian Steppes with Hans! But I worry about Brian. He could end up the abused slave."

"He already is. And Chiara will be the first to defect. After Randy puts the moves on her. He's got the sex chamber all ready—and no way Tammy can handle all those cushions on her own, or her guru's appetites."

"Oh my God! Is that what you saw when you went to the bathroom?"

Julie nodded, bursting into laughter. "He's going to handpick the community, his flock, and it's going to be heavily female."

"But with a few hefty construction workers, who are 'soft art' types but necessary for the mission's success."

"He needs pipelines to money. The flock can be bad musicians as long as they have good connections."

They laughed again.

"Are we being too mean?" Julie asked, glancing over at Jason.

"Naw, we're just having fun!"

"I can't believe we've gone from the cult of St. Francis to the cult of Randy Meister all in one day. What are you going to tell Elsa when she asks about Tammy?"

"The truth. But come to think of it, I'm not going to tell her in words, I'm going to give her a little Music Mecca painting, something deliciously occultish."

"Will it be abstract with circles and sun rays?"

"No, it's going to be figurative. It's going to show me in the cave of synchronicity at Music Mecca. Randy's going to be sitting on palm leaves on a raised platform with Tammy and me at his feet. His hands are raised to connect to divine energy, as he initiates us to the original, lost tarot and its rites. All of us are stark naked but feeling much closer to our primordial state, before the world and evil power-mongers stripped us of free will."

Julie laughed so hard that Jason squealed in warning, "Watch the road, will ya?"

"Sorry about that!"

"It was just a cliff, that's all."

"Would you mind making me a scan of the painting?"

"I won't have to; with the alchemy I learned from the abbot to-night, I can recreate one out of cow liver, but the cow has to be very young and freshly sacrificed or it won't work. And if Brian screws up with the knife, he's going to be sent to the isolation cell for naughty monks."

Julie gasped for breath and tears blurred her vision.

"For God's sake, pull over and let me drive!" Jason said. "The high priest's voodoo vesper put a curse on you! Did you see that cat they've got? Black!"

Julie made an effort to suppress her laughter, but it continued to force its way up with sudden bursts of hilarity. That was the fun of being with Jason. Finally, equilibrium was restored to the car. The headlights followed the hairpin turns with greater accuracy, and with each hill and perilous gorge safely crossed, the friends drew closer to home, an unassuming haven governed by nature.

WILD MAN

Spring came to the Sabina after months of mountain cold. It seemed to Julie as if February's full moon had warmed the night air, ending winter's bite. A few cold nights lay ahead, and capricious weather, but that was typical of March. The birds' euphoric chirping around the house signaled the change in season. Or, perhaps they were coming out of hiding now that the hunting season was over, something Julie herself was celebrating. No more startling bullets would whiz by her window. The hunters had laid down their arms so the birds and mammals could mate and produce fresh stock for future sport, for in twenty-first-century Italy hunting was for sport not family survival.

Julie set out for Collediana, a short walk around the girth of her mountain and then up the main road to the solid stone hilltown. A few farmers in the valley were still burning their annual olive-tree prunings, sending plumes of smoke into the pristine sky, but for the majority, attention had shifted to "orto," the large kitchen gardens that would supply the household with annual food, some of it jarred in the cantina. Artichokes would be the next harvest, and the bushy green plants grew not only in gardens but also along property fences, forming borders to orchards of apple, peach, and pear trees.

Spring percolated everywhere. Delicate pink cyclamen grew right underfoot on the path to town, and out on the main road, daffodils bobbed in the breeze, and bright yellow mimosa ornamented every yard. Julie had begun a watercolor album of the spring plants, recording their flowering dates at the bottom of each page. The pageant would continue until June. She now had the idea for printing a small book of Sabina plants to sell in the local gift shops.

Halfway up the hill to Collediana, Julie stopped to admire a tall tree's profusion of pale pink blossoms spreading over the road like a lace canopy. The heavenly, ephemeral cloud hadn't been there the day before. She spotted a bent and gnarled old-timer coming down the hill toward her.

"*Scusi, signore,* what kind of tree is this?" she asked.

"*Mandorlo,*" he grumbled without looking up.

Almond. But the wild almonds in her own yard hadn't bloomed yet, probably because the exposed hillside experienced fiercer wind and colder temperatures. She had found a few courageous *anemone stellata* in her upper olive grove, and white shepherd's purse, but in the valley, these wildflowers had proliferated like a ground cover, interspersed with tender shoots of grape hyacinth.

Since February's full moon and the change in temperature, Julie had begun longer neighborhood walks with Orso. The days were lengthening. What she really wanted to do was explore the ancient, rocky trails that were once the only roads between Collediana, Terni, and Rieti, but they wound through mountains in total isolation. It wouldn't be safe to hike alone, even with Orso.

The main road curved around Collediana's medieval wall and arrived at the village's hub, where school, church, bar, gas station, supermarket, post office, and other shops clustered. This sloping, unorthodox piazza was a major meeting place, as cars were not permitted inside the ancient town. Mothers drank cappuccino together every morning after dropping their children at the school.

Stonemasons began their day at the same bar with *caffè corretto,* laced coffee, while their big Iveco trucks idled outside. Every sort of morning commerce passed through this circle, causing congestion, often because two drivers stopped mid-road to roll down their windows and talk. Rarely did the cars behind them honk. This was a way of life, to stop in the middle of nonprincipal streets for a minute or two, to exchange greetings or news, and it likely predated automobiles. Julie wondered if in time cell phones would end the need for such roadway communication.

As she came up to the Antico Caffè, Julie marveled at the number of Mercedes and SUVs driven by the rural community. It was a bourgeois place—or aspired to be—despite its rustic veneer. Most mothers who brought their children to school dressed well to have their morning coffee in the bar: fashionable boots, tight pants, smart jackets, scarves, styled hair, jewelry, and designer pocketbooks.

Carolina was at the bar that morning, holding court, as Julie liked to think, for she knew everyone and all the latest news. With straight auburn hair cut along her shapely jaw and an effervescent personality full of laughter, she easily attracted friends and enjoyed putting people together almost like a mother hen. She and her husband Elio were Romans, but had decided to raise their twins outside the big city. Now, the twins had started middle-school, and Carolina worried that Collediana's curriculum wouldn't be challenging enough; she had broader, international dreams for her children. And what about her own career? If too much time elapsed she'd have trouble resuming her work as an interpreter for the foreign ministry. Her several languages and love for world travel drove her to meet and befriend the ex-pat community, and she hosted dinner parties on a weekly basis.

"Julie! I was just thinking about you and wondering if you were all right," Carolina said, as Julie entered the bar. The other women all turned to stare at the newcomer.

"I'm fine, and how's everything with you?"

Carolina quickly introduced the mothers in her coterie, who then said their goodbyes and left the bar to do their errands. Julie brought her cappuccino to Carolina's table and sat down.

Carolina was animated. "I've been trying to get you and Dottore Ruscoli together for months, and he just agreed to come for tea. Are you free? I know you'll like him—he likes books and art and he's your neighbor. His Italian is the best kind, so you can ask him about conversation lessons. He's retired and his companion is much younger and still works in Rome—she's an *avvocato*, a lawyer, so he's all alone and needs company."

Julie agreed to come. "What can I bring? Biscotti? Tangerines?"

"Don't bring anything, just yourself."

Julie's first impression of Gerolamo Ruscoli was lukewarm and she sensed it was mutual. He reeked of cigarettes, preventing her from seeing any of his attributes. During the tea, she hardly said a word. Carolina's vivacity monopolized the conversation, and Gerolamo was quick to pounce on any openings. If Julie hadn't known Carolina, she would have thought she was flirting unabashedly with her gentleman guest, to the extent of batting her eyelashes. He sat calmly in his chair at the dining-room table, dressed in the traditional male attire for social occasions: button-down shirt, pullover sweater, and corduroy pants. Italian men also took pains over their hair, and Gerolamo's thinning gray hair had been parted and combed over his balding head. His gray-white beard bristled with a fresh trim.

The tea hour passed pleasantly enough with superficial conversation in English—Gerolamo's delivered fluently with a British accent. He was some kind of nobleman, but his title wasn't mentioned, and his career had been in the government working in the department of Vatican affairs. When it was time to go, Carolina took her guests by the elbow as if to bring them physically together, "And now you two neighbors have finally met and can take your dogs for walks."

"I'd like that, come by any time," Gerolamo said politely. "No need to phone first, just show up."

Julie thanked him, adding, "I had no idea you lived at the church. I keep looking through the gate at it but always forget to go when it's open for service."

"Sant'Agnese is my only complaint about the property," he said. "I hate sharing my house with it. But I can tell you all about that when you come over."

"What about tomorrow?" Carolina beamed at them, still holding their arms. "What are you both doing tomorrow?"

"Unfortunately I have to go to Palestrina tomorrow and stay for a few days," Gerolamo said. "Business with one of my properties, it's such a nuisance, but let's plan to take the dogs for a walk early next week, whatever day is best for you."

And so it evolved that on the following Tuesday, Julie put Orso in the car and drove to Gerolamo's house. She could see his campanile from her yard, and her own narrow street, Via Sant'Agnese, ended at his house. It was named for the church since it led there.

Julie parked outside the church gate, which had a chain and padlock around it. The view through the tall, plain ironwork was romantic, showing bushy cypresses lined up on both sides of a quaint stone walkway. The trees had been there so long they almost obscured the path. Sant'Agnese's squat but classical portico stood at the end of the walk with sculptural relics in niches to each side of the green church doors.

Julie put Orso on his leash and walked up the road to the driveway entrance, where the rusted gates had been left open. There was no bell or intercom, but her footsteps on the gravel alerted Gerolamo's German shepherd to their arrival, and within seconds he was bounding toward them, barking ferociously. Orso readied himself for battle, barking back. Fortunately, Gerolamo's piercing commands came next, ordering "Zeke" to "*stai zitto!,*" shut-up. "These are our *ospiti,* Zeke, our guests." The attack was averted but not the enthusiastic greeting, for Zeke then leapt affectionately and repeatedly on Julie's chest, dragging his muddy paws down the front of her jacket and jeans.

She saw at once and with surprise that Gerolamo was not the man she had met the other day. Here in his private villa gardens he appeared a creature of the wild, grinning with glee at Zeke's bad manners and barely admonishing him to stop. He wore filthy gray pants that buttoned up the front with a few buttons missing. A bungee cord threaded through his belt loops, across his back, over his shoulder, and down his torso to fasten on the front left loop. His pants hitched up on that side, exposing his bare ankle. His green sweater under the rigging was a splotch-work of dirt, stains, and holes. Bits of twig clung to the wool. Above this ragged picture was his happy face, a Bacchus, or a gnome, pleased as punch with himself. He had not bothered to comb his hair, and his hands and fingernails were blackened from outdoor work. His right hand held lemons.

"Come in, come in!" he said with such zeal that white dots of saliva shot from his mouth, which his hand automatically waved away as if he were used to it. "You want to see the house before we walk, don't you? I sense you like old houses. And you're staying for lunch, *vero*? It won't be a grand affair but…. Don't worry, the dogs are fine—let them get acquainted. Zeke's totally meek under that roar of his!" His exuberant grin showed a row of straight teeth, probably dentures that made his speech spray.

Julie had no time to answer, he was ushering her inside, through a small untidy anteroom to the cozy kitchen, where he deposited the lemons on the table, which was a woodman's rustic construction with two chairs. Leftover food littered most of the surface—half a bread loaf with knife and crumbs around it, a few wilted artichokes, red wine in a box, and miscellaneous jars, some growing cottony mold.

"Sorry for the mess, I've been outside in the garden. Did you see my pond? I made it myself, so I could have egrets—did you see them? Every day these lucky birds get fresh fish. They live like kings. And did you see the electric fence? I had to install it to protect them after my first egret got killed, probably by a fox."

"I missed all that, sorry. How long have you lived here?"

"Five years. I'll tell you all about it. Follow me," he said, and headed back outside, his compact frame sizzling with energy. They crossed the front of the building under the portico. Two Renaissance wings flanked the older church between them. "I had expected to die when I turned fifty-six," he said.

Julie looked at him curiously.

"Yes, fifty-six. That's when my father died and his father before him. I've read all about genetics, but fifty-six came and went. I didn't die, and after four more years of waiting to die, I decided I was going to live, so I retired and moved here."

"It's healthier—"

He cut her off, "Yes, yes, but it's also fitting. You see, my paternal ancestors are from the Sabina, not far from here." He unlocked a door in the middle of an enormous glass and ironwork facade, the upper panes in a fan design. Then he stepped back to let her enter first and remained silent as she took in the room. It was rectangular with a vaulted ceiling and well-preserved biblical frescoes on the walls, the reds so crisp they could be fresh blood.

"You like it?" His voice vibrated next to her rapt face. "I bought this place for three reasons: this room, the campanile, and the church's apse, which I'll show you later—mosaics. But I had no idea the church would prove such a headache—two services a week on Saturday and Sunday. After my dogs were poisoned I stopped being nice to everyone."

"What? Someone poisoned your dogs?"

"Yes, they barked when people came to church, just as dogs do, and this bothered someone. I lost Zeke's father, and Zeke was terribly ill but recovered."

Maybe he had let the dogs jump on people, Julie thought. And had looked on without calling them off. And even smiled a little, as if he enjoyed annoying the churchgoers.

"I own the villa, but the church belongs to the town," he said, as they ascended a narrow marble staircase to a long drawing room undergoing a dusty renovation. Two adjoining bedrooms, furnished in antiques, were ready for use, and a kitchen was partially installed. "This is the wing Monica prefers," Gerolamo said. "Ah, yes, Monica… she's, er…," he hesitated. "I'm not sure which word to use in English."

"Your companion?"

"*Esatto*, my lady friend. This is her wing—it has class. But I like the other side, it's cozier. We'll go there now, through this secret door."

He opened a small door concealed in the drawing-room wall and they stepped onto the balcony above the church's nave. Julie beheld the dusty, cobwebbed interior supported by a wood-beamed ceiling. The baroque period hadn't touched it, except for the gilded Jesus above the altar.

"Lovely!" she said. "I have to come back and study it more closely."

"Of course, I hope you'll come often. And the next time I'll go down and turn on the lights so you can see the mosaics. They're priceless."

"Why is the church in the middle?"

"Originally a Roman villa stood here, then the church was built on top of it. The wings and campanile were added much later for the monks who lived here until the 1930s. Did you see my Roman walls when you drove in?"

"No."

"But you have to see them!—twelve meters high and hardly a stone missing. I removed five hundred years of thorn and ivy with my bare hands." He held them up to emphasize the work they had accomplished.

He continued talking while leading the way through an old

wood door on the opposite end of the balcony. They descended a few steps into his living quarters. This room was large, with a soaring ceiling and had been furnished with antiques to serve as both a bedroom and a den. Unlike the dingy kitchen under it, his living space exuded elegance and taste. Staid portraits of aristocrats and a few landscapes passed down from generations hung on the walls.

Julie stepped over to a window and looked down at the graceful gardens surrounding his house. Boxwood and laurel hedges divided the lawns. A terrace parapet overlooked his pond, and a pool nestled behind trees toward the back of the property. His small olive grove was on the other side of the house. Centuries-old umbrella pines and cypresses, along with the campanile, distinguished the property as a place of importance. Julie gathered how vital it was to Gerolamo to be lord of this fiefdom.

When the tour ended they set out with the dogs for a walk on a logging road up the hill from his house. In the distance elm trees gave off a reddish aura because of their tiny spring buds, and fuchsia cyclamen carpeted whole areas of the bordering woods. Birds of all varieties, many of them identified by Gerolamo, flew by, landing in trees or on the ground, indifferent to the presence of humans.

Gerolamo talked nonstop, as if he hadn't talked in weeks and had finally found an outlet. He said he had studied Greek and Latin at the classical high school, and after his university degree in history had taken business courses at Harvard. Ever since, he had kept up his subscription to the *New Yorker,* which he read faithfully each week, in addition to books on any subject. Naturally, he told her, he had pursued a career associated with the Vatican—it had been a Ruscoli tradition.

As they walked, he moved from one story to the next, tossing in French and Roman dialect for effect. He embellished his stories with arcane history, whether true or made up on the spot. Julie found it impossible to contribute; he cut off her stammering attempts. Her mind and lips couldn't work fast enough as she tried to process his deluge of information.

"I grew up near Rome's zoo," he said cheerily as they turned a corner on the logging road, "and every day my nanny, Maria, took me there, not to see the animals but to meet her lover. It was 1945 and I was three. Maria was in love with Freddie, one of your handsome American soldiers who liberated Rome. As soon as we got to the zoo, she passed me to her friend who was in charge of the chimpanzees, but he was busy, so for six months he put me in the cage with Aldo, who was exactly my age and became my best friend. Then Freddie got shipped home to Nebraska and my idyllic days with Aldo ended. It was quite upsetting, for both of us. I continued visiting him for years. But by then he hated me."

"You were free—"

"*Esatto!* As soon as he saw me coming up the walk, he'd throw himself against the cage bars and scream like a madman. If you'll pardon my rudeness, he'd pick up his shit and throw it at me."

"Ha!—And I can just see you taunting him."

"*Macché!*" His eyes widened in mock surprise, "Am I so transparent?"

She grinned at him.

On that first walk, she learned about his childhood summers at an exclusive resort in Switzerland and his teenage treks throughout Lazio and Abruzzo's mountains. When she asked about his family, his voice lowered to deliver the basics, "The Ruscolis were probably average farmers from this area, but sometime in the 1300s one of them got rich or became a priest, and the Church rewarded him with a title. Or maybe he purchased it. Eventually, one of his descendants came to Rome. One of my first memories is of my mother taking me aside and telling me in a serious way that I was never to use the word 'noble.' 'It's taboo,' she said. 'But that's what makes you different. And old furniture.'"

Without pause he launched into a story about the summer of his fourth year, when he went to his nanny's home in Umbria for her vacation. "*Her* vacation, mind you! The ancient village had no running water, and the women in the family walked down hundreds of stone steps every day to carry back water on their heads. Even at that age I watched this in amazement and noticed how I was given a bath every night, while my hosts stayed dirty. To them, I was the son of a certain Roman family…," his voice trailed off.

Back at the house, they filled tin bowls from the garden spigot for the dogs. "*Ecco! Bravi! Bevete!*" Gerolamo cheered as the dogs lapped up the water. "And now, something for us. You're staying for lunch, aren't you?"

"I'd love to, thank you."

"Don't thank me yet—I haven't shopped."

Inside the anteroom, Julie took off her muddy shoes.

"But my floor is cold!" Gerolamo protested, dropping to his knees to pull a pair of slippers out from under the bench. "Here, please, you must allow me to offer you these horrible things that should have been thrown out long ago."

"Thanks, but what about you?"

"I'll wear my muddy shoes," he grinned.

Julie clapped around the kitchen in the backless slippers and tried to be helpful, as Gerolamo made fast decisions about their lunch, his unwashed hands always in front of him, working rapidly.

"I know these artichokes look old, but I think I can rejuvenate them in a little salad," he said, peeling the three small orbs down to their hearts and then slicing them thinly. He slid the slices into a bowl of water, squirted them with lemon juice, and then dropped the lemon halves into the bowl, mixing all with his dirt-encrusted fingers. The water turned brown.

"I usually eat these raw, but today I'll cook them a little, for your benefit. Hmm, what else?" His hands found frozen peas, a handful of which he microwaved. Then he microwaved the artichokes. Meanwhile he found a bowl in the old-fashioned porcelain sink that resembled a trough. He rinsed it, barely, and brought it dripping wet to the table. In it, he mixed the artichokes and peas with lemon, oil, salt, and pepper. Then, he stared at his concoction, thinking.

"It needs a teaspoon of mayonnaise, just for texture," he said, turning to rummage in the fridge. Julie felt ravenous looking at the salad, but more was coming before they could sit down to eat: omelettes. She loved them, especially when made with freshly laid Sabina eggs.

Gerolamo talked while he cooked, moving from table to stove to sink. There were no counters in his kitchen and only a few utensils—his fingers served. Julie tried to anticipate what he might need next and quickly produce it, such as the frying pan hanging on the wall.

He was beating the eggs with a fork when his cell phone rang. He scurried to the anteroom to answer it, speaking Italian. Julie cleared the littered table as best she could. Then she found clean forks, plates, and two glasses in the drain board above the sink.

"No, no, no," she heard Gerolamo arguing into the phone, "don't be silly. I'm just making lunch! I'm not lying to you! I went for a walk, yes, with Julie and the dogs. Now I'm home and I'm making lunch. Oh for heaven's sake! Why should I lie?"

When the call finally ended he came into the kitchen, a little pink in the face but just as jovial as always, "That was Monica. She's terribly jealous, I had to calm her, but I didn't succeed. She said she's leaving Rome right now and will be here in an hour."

"Then, we'd better eat fast," Julie laughed.

"I think she's bluffing," Gerolamo said, beating the eggs again, but much faster than before. "Monica's amazing! She heard your slippers slapping the floor and said, 'Who's that?'"

"She heard the slippers?"

He nodded gleefully, "So, I had to tell her about our walk, but I swore no one was here for lunch. Are you the jealous type?"

"No." But on second thought she added, "I guess if I had a boyfriend and he was doing things with another woman I might get jealous."

"Well, Monica and I have been together ten years and that's five years too long. We're really at the end, but it's hard to cut the cord. She lives in my place in Rome, so where would she go?"

"I guess it helps that you have this place."

"Yes, but I want to end it once and for all. We haven't had sex in years, so what's she so jealous about?"

His Cheshire cat grin made Julie feel she had known him a long time, not just a few hours. The chemistry to talk, to share, to be natural and spontaneous was definitely between them, even though he did most of the talking. It didn't surprise her that earlier he had described Monica as a nontalker; who could be a talker in his company? But Julie found his chatter entertaining.

He poured egg into the sizzling frying pan and with his fingernails added chips of butter. Working fast with a wooden spatula he turned in one-fifth of the egg batter and continued folding the omelette in small sections, creating an imperfect whole but at the same time several pockets of creamy egg. The result was scrumptious. It melted in Julie's mouth, for he had told her to eat at once while he cooked his own. A moment later he joined her and began eating hungrily. But no matter how hungry, he still had to talk, his mouth full.

"I want you to meet my cousin Sofia. She studied art history and the two of you would enjoy talking."

"Great—is she in Rome?"

"Good question! She's always on the move. She started a business and brings private groups to Italy. She takes them around and then puts them up in palaces and castles where she's friends with the owners. I get invited to lunch when they come to Rome—she likes me to help entertain the ladies." He flashed a coy smile. Yes, she could see him charming the foreign visitors, especially the ladies. Sitting across from him, at such close range, she could study his face freely; his aristocratic nose with slightly flared nostrils was his best feature. If she could siphon off the puffiness from his skin, the puffiness most faces had by his age, she saw a handsome man, who must have been striking in youth when his hair and eyebrows were black, his complexion ruddy. The blue eyes had since whittled down to the lashless slits of older age, but they were merry and expressive. His head had the invincible carriage of a lion, the jaw erect and strengthened by his bristly beard. As a young man his head and face must have ranked with the marble busts of famous Romans.

Their meal was over, though he continued to sip a glass of wine, body finally relaxed. It was an Italian trait to sit comfortably after a meal and let the food digest. Many Italians stretched out for a catnap. Julie noted the bits of twig clinging to Gerolamo's sweater. He seemed to like being covered in a layer of nature—dirt, twig, leaf, and pine needle. Perhaps his wild-man appearance was a form of defiance aimed at his set in Rome. She could see him reveling in notoriety; that is, as long as he had his villa and campanile to prove his true social status.

"Am I keeping you from having a cigarette?"

"I quit, it's been a week."

"Congratulations."

"Yes, and I feel so much better. It's hard to quit when Monica chain smokes, but I'm trying, and it's not the first time either. I want to live, now that I haven't died. And I need to take care of things for Nicolò. I have to leave him something. I can't imagine him handling life on his own. He does nothing at age twenty. He's lazy. I tell him he's Oblomov—do you know who I mean?"

"Yes, I read the book. But you have to wait, he's only twenty, and boys need more time—at least till thirty."

He shook his head sadly, "But he has no talents, none at all. I try to help him think of things he might do for his career but he rejects every suggestion. I feel it's hopeless."

"He probably has other skills, like with people—what about diplomacy?"

"I already suggested it. He's actually very knowledgeable

about the world, but he rejected it. He said the entrance exam is too hard. He's the main reason I'm still with Monica, or the only reason. She's the bridge between us—on vacations, at restaurants, at family gatherings. She knows how to communicate with him and this helps me. I think he wouldn't have anything to do with me if it weren't for Monica acting as go-between."

"What about government?"

"I suggested the full range of government offices, and even the military—the officer corps of course—but," he shook his head glumly. "For now I'm going to sell the Palestrina property, which isn't easy for me. It's been in the family for four hundred years." He propped his sad face in his hands, elbows on the table, and looked at her. Slowly a smile bloomed across his face, "I'm so glad you're here! I hope you don't mind my saying so."

Julie smiled back, "I'm glad to be here, this has been a wonderful day for me."

"Don't go yet," he got up and spun around, his usual frenzy returning as he rummaged through the kitchen's disorder.

"Don't worry," Julie said, "I plan to wash the dishes before I go, so Monica sees no trace of two people for lunch."

He plunked a chocolate in a shiny pink wrapper down in front of her, "Dessert."

"What about you?"

"That's yours, eat it."

As they cleaned up and laughed about Monica's imminent arrival, Julie was aware that she was being placed in the role of "the other woman." Yet, feeling innocent and not the least bit attracted to Gerolamo as a lover, she played along. It felt so good to have a comrade, a new friend with similar interests. Before she hugged Gerolamo goodbye, they made plans to meet later in the week for another walk.

★ ★ ★

That night, like all of her nights on Monte Donato, Julie experienced the darkness. She loved solitude, but her lone perch on the mountainside changed to isolation once night fell. It was different during the day when she interacted with the valley's hypnotic beauty and the community. At night, even with a fireworks of stars for company, her hillside was pitch black and her house like a brave outpost in the depths of wilderness. It was the mountain's eerie quality that unsettled her.

A bad dream woke her up just before dawn, and she lay on her pillow forcing her eyes wide open to keep the dream from returning. But snapshots of its horrors continued to replay in her mind. She was with family and friends on the top floor of a house, which had many windows looking out on pastures ringed by mountains. A real estate agent was telling them why they should buy the property. Julie stood apart, looking out one window that faced a huge black hole in the nearest mountain. Suddenly the cavity wavered, as if a thick, menacing liquid stirred inside it. All in a split second her body sensed danger, the way animals detected the first tremors of an earthquake.

"Run!" she cried, at the same instant that the hole erupted with rock, boulders, and gases. Already gravel sprayed them indoors. Julie glanced back and saw that no one was following her down the stairs. They just stared at her. She worried that she was jumping ship, thinking only of herself, as she ran on.

She got up after the dream. It was five-thirty, and dense white fog enveloped the house, lighting her room like day. She went downstairs and ruminated over her dream while making tea. She had been reading Goethe's description of Vesuvius's eruption in 1787, in addition to current newspaper reports about the effects of climate change. That explained the explosion. Then, along the path girding Monte Donato stood a tower of craggy boulders, one balanced on top of the other. Whenever she passed that spot, she paused to look up at them and wonder if boys throughout the ages had climbed to the top. How could they resist being king of that mountain? They wouldn't think about the danger—that the rocks might tip or break off. Much of the local rock was limestone and shattered. After heavy rains, rock chunks lay in the middle of the principal roads, which had been carved from cliffs. All of these images explained her dream, but not her feelings of "jumping ship" and saving herself. Her instincts told her the dream had to do with Gerolamo, with his character and the dangers lurking for her by becoming his friend. But there was no point dwelling on it, so she put the dream aside.

Julie spent the day in her cozy studio sketching and then painting a watercolor of Gerolamo's campanile poking up through cypresses and umbrella pines. He had gone to Palestrina again, this time to show his house to a Swiss developer. Although she was perfectly content to spend the day alone, pursuing her own projects, part of her was looking forward to seeing Gerolamo again. Why else would she be making him a painting, as if she were knitting him a scarf? She wanted to please him and at the same time feel his appreciation.

Julie awoke the next morning to the sound of steady rain. Disappointment filled her—this was the day for her scheduled walk with Gerolamo. Punctually at nine he phoned, as if he'd been tapping his fingers impatiently for the proper hour to call.

"Of course we need this rain for the plants, but why it had to be today is a shame," he said. "I hope you'll come over anyway for lunch. I have a nice trout here. My egrets are going to miss their little tidbit today."

She could hear his familiar glee and gladly accepted his invitation. "I'll bring a salad."

"No, no, I have everything. I shopped on my way home from Palestrina. Your delightful presence is all that's required."

"Please…."

"Oh, all right, bring the salad. And who knows, if the rain decides to stop for even ten minutes, we can walk the dogs."

Julie's morning then became devoted to the lunch. Putting

aside all projects, she showered, dried her hair, and dressed neatly. Taking an umbrella, she headed into town along Monte Donato's path. Her neighbor Riccardo used the trail as much as she, but on horseback, so that fresh manure littered the ground. Suddenly, Julie stopped. A dead animal stretched over the embankment, its neck open showing red innards. It had beautiful russet fur and a thick tail—perhaps a fox. Then she noticed orange cord, one end tied to the animal's rear paw and the other to the trunk of a sapling. It looked like a cruel trick or torture by someone, for the cord was tight around the paw. Julie hurried on; it would take weeks for the animal to decompose. She would have to get her shovel and cover it, just as she had covered a dead kitten wrapped in someone's sweater and left on the trail a few months before. Such sights, such encounters in the woods, were part of living in the country, and their mysteries were never explained.

Julie emerged from the path and climbed the half-moon curve to Collediana. The rain suddenly changed to hail, striking cars and rooftops with the clatter of a machine-gun. She hoped her umbrella could take such a beating and half jogged the rest of the way to town. She crossed the grocery store's threshold with a gasp of relief. Her first glance told her this was not the big city: Gerolamo was there and Carolina. Gerolamo had covered his rags in an old black trench coat and wore a tweed cap to hide his hair.

"Dottore! Look who's here, it's Julie. Julie are you hiding from me? I haven't seen you in a week!" Carolina's voice rang out.

"Hey, great to see you! I've been busy painting."

"Too busy for your friends? Have you two gotten together for a walk yet? You aren't too busy for a walk, are you?"

"Carolina, which of these breads do you recommend," Gerolamo's resonant voice distracted her.

"That one—the *casareccia,* rustic. I'm planning a party for Saturday, with dancing, are you both free?"

"Unfortunately, I'll be in Rome on Saturday," Gerolamo said. "It's Nicolò's birthday and he's requested a special dinner at the

Hunter's Club."

"Next time, then," Carolina smiled, "and please bring Monica."

"Indeed! That is, if I can extract her from her law books," he laughed. "You know, she reminds me of an old tooth that the dentist is pulling his hardest to get out but never succeeds."

Carolina laughed, as Gerolamo gave a little bow to them and headed to the cash register, but not before catching Julie's eye with something close to a wink.

"Is that all you ever eat, Julie? Salad?" Carolina's voice continued to reverberate in the small shop. "I like vegetables too, but a little meat or fish is important, for protein. How do you get protein if you only eat salad?"

After a few more exchanges, Julie escaped. The hail had stopped, but the rain continued. She walked home as fast as she could, huddled under her umbrella, her bag of salad ingredients clutched to her jacket front. Her mind buzzed with thoughts, particularly how her coming lunch with Gerolamo had a clandestine feel. They weren't letting Carolina know about it. And in this small town, his neighbors would take note from behind their curtains of her repeated visits to his house. Soon, word would reach Monica that Gerolamo had "another woman," an American. Was she prepared for this gossip?

At noon, Julie drove inside Gerolamo's gates instead of parking along the public road. The rain had tapered off, but she waited inside the car because Zeke was loose and excitedly streaking her car door with muddy paws. Orso barked in the backseat. Still Gerolamo didn't come to see what all the ruckus was about. Finally Julie called his cell phone. He answered in a very quiet voice as if cupping his hand over the phone, "Monica is on the house line," he said. "She's very suspicious. She heard the dogs and wants to know who's here."

"You're kidding!"

"I know, but it's her investigative mind. She knows Zeke's bark but can tell there's another dog here. She wants to know if you're here with your dog. I can't lie, but we have to agree to the same story in case she meets you and asks. I'll be there in a minute."

He came out in his filthiest clothes, beaming from ear to ear and telling Zeke to stop all the fuss.

Julie was freed from the car and opened the back door for Orso, who bounded out and at once began slam-dancing with Zeke.

"I'm so sorry to keep you waiting! I told Monica that the alarm man had just arrived and that a stray dog had wandered in with him. She doesn't know you're here. That's the story."

"All these lies. It's getting complicated."

"Don't worry! Come in, and thank you for bringing salad. *E guarda,* Monica and I are breaking up, so it doesn't matter what she thinks. I can't take her yelling at me anymore. That's all she's done for the last five years. Yak, yak, yak—listing all my faults."

"Sounds awful. I guess ten years is the average lifespan for a relationship. Wow—the kitchen's cleaned up."

"Yes, I had the charwoman come over because of you," he said, and added with a hiss, "You Americans and your hygiene."

The dishes were washed and the floor swept, but not mopped. The same black grime from half a century coated the red tiles. At the fireplace, a fish lay on a mesh grill. Its silvery body had been covered in rosemary stalks, bay branches, and other herbs. Hot red embers waited to receive the grill, but Gerolamo was moving about with other preparations, his brain and body ratcheted to the tightest tension.

"I tried to think what vegetarians eat instead of meat, and fish seemed like a good idea."

"I'm not a vegetarian, I just like vegetables."

"I hardly eat meat myself," he said. "Have you noticed how eating meat has become right wing, almost fascist."

They laughed, and he turned back to the stove.

"See if you can find butter in the fridge," he said.

She opened the door and immediately saw a plate of cubed

beef on skewers—his next meal, when the vegetarian wouldn't be joining him. She took the butter and closed the door.

"Have you noticed that in Italian we have one word for both the animal and its meat, while in English there are two words?" he said.

"*Agnello, agnello; maiale, maiale,*" Julie said for lamb and pig.

"Brava! It all happened because of the Norman invasion, it was a French influence. There had to be cow and beef, pig and pork."

"But what about *bistecca* and *manzo*?"

"No, no, just *manzo*—steer, beef." With his fingers, he chipped butter over the fish and then put the grill into the fire. The herbs burst into flame. He quickly adjusted everything, batting down the fire with his bare hands.

"I was thinking about Italian and English while driving back from Palestrina," he said, wiping the soot from his hands on his pants. "I've figured out a major difference in how we use the jaw when speaking. We Italians really move our entire jaw around, while you English speakers keep your lips tight." He said this last sentence with severely tight lips that made her laugh. Then he demonstrated the Italians, his mouth and jaw gyrating exaggeratedly, "*Buon giorno, mio amico, oggi cosa fai?* Did you see that!" He said excitedly.

"I'm not going to go around talking like that," Julie said.

"But if you did, Italians would understand you right away." He chortled at the thought of it. "You should have seen me practicing in the car, everyone who passed me stared—What's that crazy man doing!"

He laughed again, and then dove to rescue the fish, which had caught fire. He yanked out the grill, slapped the fire out, and pushed the fish back onto the coals.

"An English person can't understand an Italian who mispronounces a vowel," he continued.

"That's true: when you said 'lawn,' the other day, I heard 'loan.'"

"*Esatto!* But it's the opposite for Italians. If you mispronounce a consonant, we have no idea what you're saying. Vowels are flexible for us, we accept them in almost any form, but not consonants, those are rigid. The *pesce* is ready, Madam, and if you pronounce it like *pes-kay,* an Italian will think you're saying peaches instead of fish."

They sat down to eat. Salt was in a tin can for fingers to pinch and pepper was in a mortar and pestle. Gerolamo jumped up a few more times for forgotten items, a half-empty bottle of unlabeled wine and some warmed-up potatoes in the microwave oven. He deboned the fish, oblivious to his sooty hands. Did he ever wash his hands? Julie wondered. Were his dirty hands an act of defiance, like his clothes? She would just have to forget that his hands had been all over the dog, dog food, household dirt, the garden, and of course the bathroom.

"*Buon appetito.*"

"*Buon appetito.*"

"I'm sorry the egrets did not get their fish today," Gerolamo said, happily munching the fish's tasty white flesh. "Their sacrifice for you shows good judgment—they'll be well rewarded tomorrow."

Julie thanked him and asked if his father had also liked to cook.

"No, no, we had help for that. I learned later, because I liked to eat and had the interest. My father liked to talk, that was his specialty. He was *allegro,* always cheerful and sociable. As a child, I identified with my mother's family—they were university people, lawyers. It was only after my father died that I began to identify with him. I had to fill his shoes, manage affairs for my mother. I remember one of my first actions. For years my father had a mistress, Stefania, and after his death, I told my mother we must go see her, it was the proper thing to do. So we paid her a visit and all cried together."

"Did your father have a career?"

"Oh, yes—he was in the Pope's guard—the Guardia Nobile. It doesn't exist anymore, but it was prestigious. I remember his uniform—exquisite! The helmet alone was something extraordinary. An entire horsetail hung down from a gold horn in the crest of the hat. And the boots! Black and polished, drawn up over the knees. The red jacket shone with epaulets. It had buttons and belts going this way and that. He wore white gloves. So, now you understand why my mother fell in love with him—here was a *man!* Once in St. Peter's Square an American soldier came up to him and said, 'Are you a cardinal?'" Gerolamo laughed heartily, "It was the red jacket, but oh—'are you a cardinal?'"

"It would take an American. Did you save his uniform?"

He shook his head, "He was buried in the regular blue one. They didn't waste the red ones on coffins. We had to give it back. Then, many years later when my mother died, I had to move the family bones around to fit her in. I saw my father's femur. It was big, like this, and perfect! It was an incredible femur. At that moment I felt so proud to be descended from such a femur as that. The gravedigger picked up a scrap of the cloth from the uniform and rubbed it between his fingers: *'Rrrrroba der Vaticano,'* he said in Roman dialect, 'stuff of the Vatican.'" But my poor father, his last suffering days were the happiest of my life, up until then. My mother was in the hospital most of the time, doing what she could for him. I was sixteen and suddenly totally free, as if the prison gates had opened. A friend and I stole the car and drove all over Rome. We picked up our first whores! What a spree!" Julie looked at his exultant face; it was as if he expected her to congratulate him for picking up whores.

The phone rang and he jumped to get it, while Julie continued to think about his "first whores"—which implied subsequent whores. What kind of man visited whores and squealed with delight about such cavorting, as if it were a legitimate rite of passage? Was this an Italian or a European tradition? What was his moral code? In fact, she could hear him now on the phone with Monica, bleating defensively, but also passive-aggressively that "no, no, no, he was having lunch all alone today, a stale panino with leftover ham that was starting to smell. The gardener had just arrived to prune the trees, and the alarm man said he would have to come back another day because he needed a part."

The conversation then fell to a whisper, with words like "documents," "property," and "work" repeating. Finally he returned to the table and an awkward silence followed. But as he cleared the dishes, his usual pep rekindled, "You could hear who that was! She was having a temper tantrum."

"Because I'm here?"

"No, or not just that. To make a long story short, in the past she's been kind enough to help not only me but also my cousin—the art historian I told you about—with the legal documents whenever Sofia buys property. But now she's bought a Barberini palace on the Tuscan coast, and Monica says that's it! She won't handle it—Sofia's affairs on top of mine, in addition to her regular job—she says she's been pushed too far."

"Does Sofia pay her?"

His gray head wiggled noncommittally, "It's always been a family favor, she gets a lot in return, believe me—my access—but I told her this time she should bill Sofia. The truth is she just likes to complain. I know she has the time, but she's mad at me and likes to vent at every opportunity."

"I hope you two can work it out for better or worse."

"Me too. It's come to that point. I have to break it off." He sat back down with a glum expression, but then his eyes met hers and his smile returned, "I love looking at your face. I'm so glad you're here! Please, don't rush off, let me make you tea. And tomorrow, if the weather's good, we can take that hike to the sanctuary."

That night, Julie was relieved to be in her own space and worried that Gerolamo might invade it with a phone call or an impromptu visit. All in a week, an intense whirl, they had become friends. True, they had only cracked the surface of each other's lives, but the chemistry to spend time together was strong, palpable. She wanted to resist it but saw she was doing the opposite. Even though she had no desire to touch him, she knew from experience that soon enough this would change. A man and a woman spending hours and days together, eventually stayed together. And his life was in turmoil—an ex-wife in one palazzo, a mistress in another, a son with maturing issues, and his own constant financial worries. He lied effortlessly and used people, such as Monica for his legal affairs. Julie sensed he was also assessing her, for over their tea following lunch he had asked about her property and how she managed to live without a job. He had prodded for details—Alan's death and legacy, her own prospects. Was he looking for a companion who wouldn't drain his scant resources, or even better, one who could share his expenses? Already he had suggested that she share his gardener. Other things about him set off her internal alarms. She suspected he thrived on complicated liaisons with women. Hadn't she learned about the lifestyle of the aristocracy from reading Malaparte's *Kaputt*? Affairs were mandatory amusement for both men and women if they wanted a reputation; triangles were a game, a competition. Intrigues kept life titillating no matter how emotionally painful when they imploded. But Julie's greatest concern was for her love of silence, solitude, and work; Gerolamo was constant commotion, the center of attention. With him she would always be doing what he wanted and never fulfilling her own goals. His hyper personality and mercurial, dishonest lifestyle would smother her and ultimately outrage her. And she mustn't forget she rejected everything he stood for—nobility, entitlement, and perpetuation of an elite class. For centuries Rome's titled families had vied for positions in the papacy in order to increase their family's landholdings and wealth, always at the expense of peasants and the rest of society, even at the expense of each other, their blood relations, for they had killed each other off viciously for power. True, they had also been patrons of the arts and that legacy was invaluable; yet, the motives behind such collections and commissions had been, in most cases, grossly self-serving. No, Gerolamo and his ingrown, self-important world were not for her; country living had thrown them together and she should watch out.

Reciting these cautions to herself had no effect on Julie. While the litany played on in her mind, she was anticipating the next day's hike, what she would wear, and what questions she would ask Gerolamo about his life and the Sabina's history. Her watercolor of his campanile was ready, and that night, with relaxing music on, she made a card to go with it: a pen-and-ink sketch of an olive tree with her friendly message printed below it. She knew she was acting like a teenager in love, only she wasn't in love, she was fascinated.

Wind woke her at four in the morning. Her bedroom shutters banged and she got up to fasten them. Howling gusts were coming from the north, but she hoped they would subside by late morning so that she and Gerolamo could go on their hike. At seven, wind still ripped across her exposed hill, although the sky was cloudless and the sun intended to rise. She went about her usual routine until nine, when Gerolamo called.

"What do you think?" he said in a mouselike voice, the one he used for confidences.

"It's windy, but it could get better. We could wear layers."

"Good!" He perked right up to his usual full throttle. "The wind is fine with me. Let's leave late morning to take full advantage of the sun. I'll pack a few things for a picnic. Don't bring anything, I have enough here."

They hung up and Julie imagined him throwing on his black trench coat and jumping into the car for a quick trip to the grocery store. She went downstairs to the kitchen to find a bag for her painting and laid it on the table while she rummaged the cabinets.

A sing-song voice startled her, and over her shoulder she

saw Carolina traipsing down the outside stairs to the glass doors. "Hello, Julie!" Her fashionable scarf whipped in the wind, and her hands futilely brushed hair from her face as she stooped to pick up a potted plant that had blown over on the patio. Julie hurried to let her in.

"Carolina!"

"Good morning, Julie, what wind on Monte Donato! Much worse than in Collediana. I'm on my way to Rome—a lucky interpreting job, someone got sick. I wanted to drop this off for you."

It was a loaf-shaped cake covered in cellophane. She put it down on the table and spotted Julie's watercolor, "Oooh! How pretty! Isn't that Dottore Ruscoli's campanile? Are you two finally having some fun together? He's an interesting man, isn't he? I knew you'd like him. And I don't think he and his companion are...getting along that well."

"Thank you for this cake!"

"It's not cake—it's made with polenta, hardly any sugar. I thought you'd like it. What are you doing today?"

"The usual. I was waiting for the wind to die down so I could take Orso for a walk. Then, a little work, some reading, maybe a swim."

"Hmm, no social life today? You need to get out more, see your friends. I hope you're still coming for dinner and dancing tomorrow night."

Julie's innards dropped but she kept smiling. She had hoped the party plan had fizzled out. She wanted to be all by herself when she wasn't walking or eating lunch with Gerolamo. The usual ex-pat crowd would be there, and William would try to flirt, put his hands on her. But perhaps Umberto the journalist would be there, if he wasn't traveling, and she liked him. She could plunk down next to him for the entire evening.

"Yes, thanks, you're so good to always get people together."

"I like to and I miss dancing. When Elio and I were courting we danced every night." She swung her hips and laughed, looking girlish and pretty. "Who would have known what a imbecile he'd turn out to be!" She picked up the watercolor. "I just love this! Will you paint my house sometime?"

"Of course, I love your front door with all the flowerpots—I've been wanting to paint it. Let's do it in a few weeks when spring's peaking."

"Perfect! I'll have time to get all the plants in shape, and I'll add your orchid!" Carolina hugged Julie. "Thank you, *cara!* And see you tomorrow, don't cook anything, bring a bottle of wine if you want."

Julie waited ten minutes before setting out for Gerolamo's. She worried that Carolina might still be in the neighborhood, chatting through her car window with a friend who happened to be passing in the opposite direction. Finally, feeling surreptitious, Julie drove the exposed road to Gerolamo's and felt relief to pass through his gates into the villa's concealed realm.

Gerolamo was in the kitchen in a frazzled state, moving to and fro with picnic preparations. He hardly lifted his head to greet her and seemed distracted. Perhaps Monica had just called.

"We can cook these over the fire," he said, thrusting two balls of aged mozzarella cheese—scamorza—into the knapsack on the table. His hands were as dirty as always. "And wine, we have to have wine."

"Here, I have a little present for you."

He stopped, surprised. "For me? What is it?" He took Julie's small painting out of the gift bag and stared down at it. "*Carino!*" He stared some more, checking for details, "I love it! Thank you, Julie." He propped it on the mantelpiece and gave it one more close look. "And there was a letter!" He turned back to the bag.

"You can read it later—it's just a card."

"No, I want to read it now." He pulled it out, "*Favoloso! Guardi questi bellissimi olivi!* Julie, you're fantastic!" His eyes skimmed the friendly sentiments and then looked at her with appreciation. He propped the card tenderly next to the painting.

"You'd better throw it out so Monica doesn't see it."

"Not yet, I want to keep it for a few days. I'm so tickled."

He came back to the table. "What a surprise! But so like you. You brighten things up, I want to keep you here." His body spun around, his eyes scanning objects, "What else do we need? Oh, yes, the wine!" He grabbed a box of orange juice, shook it, heard sloshing at the bottom, and quickly drank off the remains directly from the nozzle. Then he poured wine from an open bottle into the juice box, but not much was left, so he added more wine from a different bottle. Then he capped the box. "That'll do it. What else?"

"I don't need a big picnic."

"An orange!" He tossed it in. "I have only one but we can share it. And how about *fagioli*?" He threw in a small carton of cannellini beans that could be cut open like an individual cereal box. Then he took a dirty paring knife from the sink, wrapped it in newspaper, and thrust it in the knapsack, along with a packet of biscuits for the cheese. Julie tore off a few paper towels and added them to the bag. Gerolamo paused to tally his efforts, then said, "Something to heat the beans!" He dashed off into the pantry, returning with a tin camping pan, which he sniffed skeptically. "Leftover from my army days, but still good, I think." He pushed it in, not bothering to rinse it. Julie fully expected to catch a virus after eating this meal.

"We're ready!"

But halfway down the driveway they had to return for a lighter to start the fire.

Finally they were off, driving a rugged dirt road a few kilometers into the mountains, the dogs alert with anticipation in the back seat. Julie looked at her companion's profile. He had put on a toddler's baby-blue knitted hat with a tassel bobbing in the back and long strings dangling against his beard.

She chuckled.

"*Che c'è?*" he said, eyes twinkling at her.

"You look bizarre in that hat! It looks like a baby's bonnet."

"It was Nicolò's. I couldn't find anything else." He grinned at her as he drove, relishing his bizarreness. She thought he was a maniac, rushing towards this picnic in a driven, euphoric state, as if it were his destiny—the fire, the cheese, the outdoor adventure, and a captive woman.

They began their trek on a logging road, and after ten minutes he said they had missed the trailhead. Telling her to follow, he bushwhacked straight up the side of the mountain, under nets of prickly tree limbs and through ankle-deep leaves mixed with craggy Sabina rock. Sometimes he clawed his way on all fours over steeper terrain, and she realized she had greater balance, or perhaps it was their ten-year difference. The dogs had no problem dealing with the wilderness, but they must have wondered what was going on. Julie trusted Gerolamo, but during that arduous climb that lasted twenty minutes she found her thoughts drifting more than once to suspicion: What if he has some sicko plan and I've been naïve enough to walk right into it?

Finally, with Gerolamo pink in the face and a bit breathless, they hoisted themselves over a final ledge onto a solid path. "I knew we'd hit it eventually. I'm very sorry about putting you through that endurance test," he said. "And what a lady—not a word of complaint! If it had been Monica…well, I would be shot in the head by now."

Julie didn't answer but opened herself up to the wonderful trail, full of birds. It followed a deep channel between mountains that long ago must have been a river, a gushing, torrential river, because the wind traveling down the chasm roared in her ears, much like water. The woods were full of beech and holm oak, and a sea of brown leaves covered the steep forest floor. The trail, an ancient road to another hilltown thirty kilometers away, was narrow and cut from white limestone. The sanctuary was about five kilometers away. Gerolamo wanted to picnic there. When they passed a wide swath of denuded land, shaped like a bowl, he paused to explain why the lumberjacks had left behind a handful of scrappy trees.

"It's called *matricina*," he said. "These 'little mothers' will re-populate the forest."

"And look at Soratte!" Julie said. The majestic mountain, always a bluish silhouette with five distinctive peaks like saw teeth, dominated the Sabina landscape the way Vesuvius dominated Naples.

"Ah! I love that sight!" Gerolamo said. "*Vides ut alta stet nive candidum.* We had to memorize Horace in high school."

"What does that mean?"

"*See how resplendent in deep snow Soratte stands. Vides ut alta stet nive candidum,*" he repeated. "It's incredible, I can still remember what I learned in high school, but I can't learn anything new. My brain is finished."

They resumed hiking single file, he leading.

Julie talked to his back, "I read in the newspaper that seniors can improve their memories by learning new things instead of following their usual routines. I think you should buy a computer and learn to do research on the internet—it could ward off senility."

"No, no, it's hopeless. I don't have a brain left." He stopped and turned around to face her, smiling as always. "When I didn't die ten years ago, I was convinced there was something wrong with me and it would show up any day. I couldn't stand the suspense, it was eating away at me. So finally, I called one of my medical friends, and he ran every possible test, including a complete body scan. That's when I saw my cortex, there was nothing left of it—it was this big!" He held up his thumb and forefinger in a tiny circle.

"The size of a pea?"

"*Brava!* So after that experience and the severe depression that followed, I retired to finish out my days here. And now that I've quit smoking—and found you—I feel I might live forever!"

A terrific gust of wind knocked them off balance. "Let's go, we're right in the path of the wind," Julie said.

"The trail turns east in a little bit—we'll see if the wind follows us."

In another half hour they came to an oak grove that protected a meadow. A shepherd was crossing the open land with a small herd of sheep and a few dogs. They all waved a hand to each other. It was sunny and windless in the meadow, but Gerolamo checked his watch and said it was too early for lunch; besides, he wanted to reach the refuge, he was determined.

They left the meadow on a dirt road that ascended a new hill, and soon enough the whipping wind pummeled them. One of the shepherd's dogs had followed them and it was useless to shoo her away, for she had adopted them, or Zeke. The two of them trotted along together, sniffing and tasting each other's not so private parts, and smiling happily. The female, who might have had some boxer blood, kept her short tail straight up as if inviting closer inspection, and Zeke was only too happy to oblige.

After another hour of hiking they reached the magnificent sanctuary, a broken-down ruin with high walls occupying a cliff top. The sheer drop was staggering.

"Why did monks like to live like that—facing a sheer drop?"

"It made it easier to throw out heretics. *Buon Dio!* Look at Zeke!" he cried. The dogs were mating. "It's his first time! He's not even one and this is his first time! Good boy! Congratulations!" It was over quite fast but then the dogs found they couldn't come apart. They were glued together. They did a slow dance around the rocky mountainside trying to disengage, but to no avail. Their ginger steps finally led them to be stuck almost rear to rear, and that's how they remained, awkwardly following the others up the less steep side of the sanctuary's promontory.

"I remember this phenomenon," Gerolamo called out against the terrific wind that came down on them from the summit as if warning them not to trespass any further. "He can't get out. He has to wait for his 'you-know-what' to subside. It takes at least twenty minutes, maybe longer. Good boy, Zeke! *Bravo!* How was it? It was your first time, *complimenti!*"

"How are we going to build a fire up there in this wind?"

"We'll use the wall—bring some sticks with you."

They began collecting sticks as they made their way up to the ruin. It was a spectacular spot, the closest thing to being in the sky, with lower mountains ringing their perch in every direction. "What did they eat up here? How did they survive?"

"Sheep, chickens, wildlife, a few fruit trees, olives, *vino,* plenty of vino."

"What about water?"

"They had to walk for it, but not far, there's a spring over there. They had mules. I'm going to start this fire."

He went to a corner of the ruin and worked with sticks and newspaper to light the fire. It was too windy, too cold. He moved back into the shrubs behind the ruins and started over, calling out to Julie to find leaves because he had used up the newspaper.

She entered his shrubs with an armful of leaves. He was on his knees fighting with the fire, teeth gritted. It meant so much to him.

"Don't worry about the fire. Can't we eat the cheese the way it is?"

"It won't taste right." For once he wasn't talking much and his curt tone made her steer clear of him. She unpacked the picnic and went off for more sticks and leaves. The dogs were still stuck, but patient. Orso stood by watching the scene, the odd man out.

The next time Julie returned, the fire was smoking and a few leaves were red around their edges, having lit but died out. Gerolamo took her offerings and as usual worked with his bare hands, even when the fire caught, moving twigs around in flames as if his hands were tongs.

Julie's hands were numb from the wind. She wanted to eat and get off that mountain. She didn't think he wanted to impress her with the campfire—a romantic idea—but rather was intent on eating his scamorza cheese. As if confirming this he told her to find two long sticks for the cheese balls. A small fire was now crackling, and he found the sticks himself, peeling off their twigs to make skewers. He pierced one cheese on each stick and handed both to her, "Toast them the way you Americans do marshmallows—not in the fire but very close, so the cheese inside melts. And don't let them drop off the stick once they begin to melt."

While she held the cheeses over the flames, he began his other preparations for their rustic meal, lamenting that he had forgotten forks. He heated the beans in the army tin and tore the empty box to serve as a plate for his own portion, as Julie would get the pan. She hoped the beans in their slimy liquid would cook and cook until all germs had been killed. Those chef's hands had been patting not only Zeke and Orso, but also the new dog, who lived with sheep. And where had the dogs' tongues just been?

Finally they ate in primitive fashion standing up. The cheese was good, soft and gooey. Gerolamo bit into his ball right from the stick, but Julie used her fingers to pull off bites. When the beans were steaming, Gerolamo divided them and drank his off from the torn box. He swigged wine to wash down the food. This was the life he loved; not even simplicity but caveman conditions. The dogs were now separated and joined Orso near the food, waiting for any scraps. Only the beans were leftover, as Gerolamo had finished Julie's cheese ball, exclaiming, "I haven't eaten this much mozzarella in forty years!"

His face was red, either from exertion or wind, but he was fed and satisfied, his mission accomplished. Julie began to clean up, repacking the knapsack. "I look forward to getting out of this wind," she said.

"Me too, but wait, I have to take just one minute to see this view before we leave," he said, heading for the precipice.

"I can see it from here," Julie said, knowing how her head swam when she stood at cliff edges, or even in church domes, and looked down. "Be careful!"

He was scrambling over bits of walls to reach the best vantage point of all, where an immense yellow rock jutted out over the gulf like a diving board. Gerolamo stood on it facing the view, thin legs planted slightly apart and arms stretched wide as if to bare his chest, his soul, to the magnificence of nature, the wonder of life. He looked back at Julie and swung his arm at her, "Come here, you have to see this!"

With a heavy heart, she agreed, she would have to see it, have to share the culminating moment with him. Indeed, his arm was still outstretched to receive her. She made her way over the stones, thinking how her steps were leading not just to the perilous view, but also to the next stage of their relationship, for when she reached him, his arm would encircle her, protect her from her fears. He would kiss her. She scrutinized his face; his smile blazed under the ridiculous blue bonnet, perhaps masking his own fears about his conquest.

She was two meters from his hand when the earth vibrated under her feet. She saw Gerolamo on his wedge of rock crack away from the mountain, as a single entity—rock and man. She saw clearly surprise, disbelief, confusion, and outrage passing over his features at once. She felt horror and shock—his and hers—as they looked at each other. For split seconds he stood as if on a magic carpet, until the rock dropped faster and he was swimming in the air, swimming to reach land or a tree limb to grasp, swimming frantically back to the cliff, but not traveling forward, only down, without even time to scream in panic, for all the forces of his mind were concentrated on surviving. The distant sound of the rock crashing through trees and splintering apart on land was like a bomb exploding or an avalanche annihilating everything in its path. More sounds followed, the fallout of rolling rocks, breaking twigs, rustling leaves, animals and birds leaping for safety. Then, all was silent, more than silent; all was paralyzed and aghast, surreal. Julie stood unmoving, unbreathing, before the untouched landscape that revealed no trace of the cataclysm that had just happened. Instead, uncannily, perfect serenity spread from the blue sky and bright sun. She heard Zeke bark, a single query. A gust of wind slapped her back. "My God!" she gasped, "My God!" The dogs began to stir at the sound of her voice. Helpless, frantic, drowning in unreality, she scurried down the accessible side of the promontory, her mind screaming that she should look for him but no, she should run home for help first. At the base of the cliff, in the gorge, she saw no trace of broken rock or human remains among the trees and thorns, but there were acres of ground to cover. She looked up and immediately saw, high up, his blue bonnet dangling from a crooked tree that grew perpendicularly from the cliff face. Then she saw him, curled in the gnarled tree roots fastened to the mountain—they could tear from the crumbling limestone at any moment. How had he scrabbled his way there in the swift seconds of his descent? But there was no time to wonder. And surely he was gravely injured.

"Gerolamo! Gerolamo!"

"*O Dio,*" his faint voice drifted down to her like a falling leaf. "*Sono morto!*"

Heart bursting, limbs wired to fly, she yelled back, "Don't move! Not for anything, not for hours! I'm going for help. Everything will be all right."

"*Brava, piccola, sei un angelo.*"

END OF SUMMER

Suddenly it was the last week of August and summer was ending. The evenings cooled dramatically, and in ten more days Collediana's only outdoor pool would be too cold for Julie's regular swim. In the worst heat of July, the water had been tepid and as cloudy as soup. But mostly the baking hot days had been wonderful—dry, breezy, fragrant with jasmine, and full of anticipation for the ripening olive crop.

That Saturday at the tail end of August, the first rain in eight weeks came. Half-hearted thunder preceded it like the low rumble of indigestion, while the sun still shone everywhere except over Soratte where dark sky hovered. It seemed more than possible that the longed-for wetting of earth and trees would fail to happen. But as the sun lowered toward the horizon pinkening its distant meeting of land and sky, the first drops came in the size of quarters and made a distinct patter on Julie's brick terrace and a more sizzling, dusty sound in the driveway. From the kitchen porch, Julie watched the golden shower of Zeus enveloping Danaë in the divine love that produced Perseus, one of her childhood heroes. Everywhere, delicate olive branches lifted and waved, like hummingbird wings, reaching for a taste of those life-giving drops. Julie beamed at the rain and trees and imagined her farming neighbors doing the same, their weathered faces turned up to the sky, their wide grins rejoicing with "Alleluia!" Although hot summers were fine for the olive crop, eight weeks without rain threatened the fruit's juiciness. Julie's olives, grown on rocky slopes, were the first to wrinkle like aging skin. The fat plump nuggets of early July had shriveled to bone, or pit, though Mario had said they'd recover if the rain came soon.

The soft shower ended all too fast, and the earth dried off in the sun's last rays, filling the cooling air with the pleasant smell of mixing plants—fennel, mint, grass, lavender, and trees. A lovely evening lay ahead, a garden party celebrating the end of summer. A restaurant a few towns away was hosting the event for the owners' friends. Carolina had invited Julie, Umberto, and Dr. Gradi. Carolina's irascible husband Elio was friends with the restaurant's owner—they worked out at the same gym.

Parties were ubiquitous in the summer. Throughout the Sabina, the medieval villages hosted *sagra*, festivals, celebrating all kinds of traditions from *stringozzi*, the eggless pasta invented during wartime, to prosciutto, medieval costumes, saints, and of course *La Famiglia*. Competing posters at crossroads and on town billboards announced upcoming sagras. Every weekend the townspeople could count on a thriving outdoor party replete with music and fireworks in one of the hilltowns. These lively scenes reminded Julie that the Italians loved to gather outside, even in winter, and talk for hours. As a society, overall, they didn't go to parties with the intention of getting drunk, in contrast to partygoers in the States. They went to mingle, to socialize. Also, in the humble farming community private parties had never been a tradition. They cost too much, in resources and time, and the family meal was the main social scene. The communal party, subsidized by the town, allowed hard-toiling residents to see other townsfolk at small cost—a few euros for a plate of food and drink. The festival traditions reinforced the unique traits of Italian culture, anchored to family as an all-in-one economic and social unit, and contributed to the invisible screen that prevented progressive influences from the outside world—the bane and beauty of Italy in the new millennium.

Julie dressed up for the first time that summer, for most country gatherings were casual. She put on a polished cotton dress and jewelry. Her sandals were new. She stopped in front of the mirror several times to admire herself, for it wasn't often she looked so feminine.

With the sun still setting over the cooling landscape, Julie drove to Umberto's house, where she would leave her car and go to the party in his. Carolina and Elio were bringing Dr. Gradi from Collediana in their car. Everyone conserved gas by carpooling and even shopping together, if the distance was long.

Driving in the Sabina was always a pleasure. The roads wound through farmland with ancient stone dwellings surrounded by colorful plants. One picturesque view flowed into the next. Julie passed Gerolamo's hedged-in villa with its campanile poking up—the flag of an aristocrat. He had recovered from his terrible fall, and the close call had made him rethink his waning relationship with Monica. He had run into Julie in the grocery store some time after his discharge from the hospital. "They've reined me in, Julie," he babbled in his old way, "Monica and Nicolò won't allow it anymore. They told me I live like a wild man and it's bad for my reputation in Rome. Nicolò took me aside and pleaded with me not to end things with Monica. 'Papa,' he said, 'where are you going to find someone else at your age to take care of you when you're dying?' He was right, and I was proud of his wisdom." His grin took over his whole face.

"Good, Gerolamo, I'm glad it's all working out," Julie had answered, and they hadn't run into each other since.

The road curved sharply, but Julie managed to watch the scenery in short snatches. The summer's baking heat had left the fields a soft tan after July's hay-cutting. Olives still embroidered the hillsides, often in neat diagonal rows, and holm oak and elm created dense patches of green at regular intervals. Grapes grew along wires stretched between wooden posts, reminding her that this year she would plant her own vines. Suddenly a field of brown sunflowers stretched endlessly. It was a shock to see those scorched heads hanging down as if from a noose, when only a month before their uplifted faces had blazoned the world with golden joy. Soon a machine would come along and shake the seeds from those pitiful burnt heads.

Umberto was a media man, his stone farmhouse outfitted for his communications outpost—satellite dish, wireless antenna, phone line, and inside four computers and a widescreen TV that was always tuned in to world news. In his early sixties and living alone, Umberto ate too much and exercised too little but carried his weight with a distinguished air, aided by his height and clean, pressed clothes. He had a head of gorgeous silver hair that waved elegantly in the right places, and his white beard was light—the going fashion among artistic types. He was descended from several European nationalities and spoke German, French, Italian, and English effortlessly. He had elected to be a Swiss citizen for pension purposes—having worked for Swiss companies—and made frequent trips to Switzerland. But he owned no property there, and none of his relatives had been Swiss. He loved to be on the road and had religious contacts in several countries where he could count on luxurious accommodation. He had a passion for new technology, and the old wood staircase going to his second floor was cluttered with these devices, as if he had tried them out and then abandoned them. His checkered career still baffled Julie; each time she met him he described another job he had once had, including company management, market research, consular affairs, cruise ship tours, and his mainstay throughout his life, journalism about the Vatican. For the past few years, he had been covering the inside scoop on church politics for a secret patron in the Hague, who sold the stories as a newsletter to a large clientele. Julie imagined something along the lines of an opposition voice, or even a scandalmonger rag. Umberto had his contacts, or informants, who in their priestly robes adorned with a gold cross sought revenge on their adversaries, and Umberto leaked the outrage. Or so Julie imagined. She liked her hyperenergetic friend immensely; he was a good man. Often he babbled faster than she could think, but from the outset they had talked freely, sharing the same perceptions about people or occurrences in the Sabina and their ex-pat circles. It didn't matter that their actual worlds were nothing alike, for Umberto was deeply involved in and committed to the Catholic Church and Julie was nonreligious. Anxious over his age and small Swiss pension, Umberto was flirting with the possibility of joining a Teutonic order in Germany, where the ruling bishop knew about his controversial church reporting but still welcomed him. Negotiations were underway about his candidacy for a lay position in the monastery.

Julie found Umberto standing in his farmyard ready to go as she pulled in and parked next to his vintage black vehicle that looked like a cousin to the Hummer.

"So, you are trusting me to drive you to dinner in my police car," he said as she got out of her car. "Are you sure you don't have second thoughts?"

They hugged the perfunctory way. "I'll take my chances, especially because I'm starved," Julie said.

"Same, let's go."

It was a high step up to the passenger seat and the leaden door took four tries to latch. The engine was clanky and the clutch or transmission threatened to drop in the road in low gear. But Umberto obviously loved the muscle it took to turn that wheel and make the real wheels obey. He took a rugged back road to join the main road, gassing it as the jeep plunged down a stony ravine to cross the ford of a dry river bed.

"This is why I come this way," he laughed. "And don't think that river is always stones like that—in winter it's flowing. Last March, I came through it in my Fiat and got stuck in the middle. Gianni had to come and pull me out with his car." Sometimes horses pulled cars or trucks out of ditches—Julie had witnessed it.

Umberto went on telling her about his new vehicle, how he'd been swindled buying it, how it consumed gas, but how remarkable it was because he could push a button and switch from his natural gas tank to his unleaded tank. But most of all he liked being in an old police car and watching the effect it had on people as he drove by. The old *carabinieri* seal on the doors could still be seen through the black paint covering it. Julie felt she was riding across rough terrain in a shockless, grinding jeep, and might bump her head on the ceiling if she didn't hold on to her seat.

They passed through Rocchette, one of the Sabina's most evocative towns, rising off its jagged rock to a pinnacle of ancient towers. Steep ravines surrounded it on all sides. On the small hill behind it perched Rocchettina, with its single castle ruin adding to the area's mysterious allure. Julie had visited the caving-in place, whose broken walls offered no protection from the dangerous cliffs. Visitors were free to comb the site with its imploding mortar and beams of former rooms, and it was this utterly natural state of the ruin that made it so thrilling, so tangibly connected to the past.

As Umberto drove through Rocchette's narrow junction at the base of its hill, the townspeople milling there fastened their eyes on his police car. An ancient stone trough with water flowing continuously from a spigot was their central meeting place.

"Rocchette has the best water in the region," Umberto said, "have you tasted it yet?"

"Not yet," Julie said, meeting the eyes that followed the police car as it bumped and clanged past. Her first weeks in the Sabina, she had been startled at how the local people stared at her or anyone who happened to pass by on foot or in a car. Everyone was everyone's business, particularly strangers. The word for foreigners in Italian was *stranieri,* strangers. But even people from neighboring towns were viewed as outsiders. Each hilltown had its own isolationist identity. Italy's ancient tradition for feuding between both neighbors and villages had continued to the present time.

Umberto gassed it as soon as he passed his audience. He pointed to cross streets and told Julie where they led and what points of interest you could find along them. His restless, roving spirit made him know all the roads for hundreds of kilometers. He liked to stop and meet shop proprietors, discuss business with them and also their family histories. He told Julie about the salami factory near Rocchette, the lumberyard with solar panels on the road to Arezzo, and the winery outside Assisi—all of which he would show her one day. Driving and meeting people—especially restaurant owners—was one of his social outlets.

"Hey, do you know about Music Mecca?" Julie said.

"No, what is it?"

"It's down that road on your left. It's in the abbey."

"Someone's living in the Cistercian abbey?"

"Yes—an American guru who's organizing an artists' commune. They're looking for funders to restore the building. They want to grow their own food and support a musicians' residency program."

"I'll have to check it out. Sounds like a story."

"Wait till I tell you more about it."

"Ohhh, so it's not just a straightforward hippie commune…."

"Is any commune straightforward?"

"Ha—all the better. I can't wait, tell me more about it now."

And so she did, for the next five kilometers until they arrived at their destination, one of the last Sabina towns before the autostrada's black gash through the center of Italy. They parked and climbed a few steps to an iron gate that led into a beautiful garden set-up for a wedding, every detail sparkling with anticipation for the coming event. Tables and chairs draped in white linen formed an arc around both a patio and a lawn ornamented with palms, magnolias, lush shrubs, and fragrant climbers. This Garden of Eden ended at a cliff where the velvet lawn rolled over the edge like a waterfall. There, at that spot, the last dusty glow of sunset filled the sky like the backdrop of a painting, with undulating hills and farmland resting peacefully under the heavens. A band was setting up on a platform at this location, and Julie and Umberto, early arrivals, strolled toward the precipice while taking in their surroundings.

They were starved and there would be no drinks or snacks until the party started. Snacking before an Italian meal took up space in the stomach, and space would be needed for the banquet. Drinking accompanied dining—it was not a predinner warm-up. The family-run restaurant was known not only for its superb food, but also for its modest prices. The owners could be seen through a glass facade in the dining room checking the final details. The chef, a plump forty-year-old country woman, wasn't anything like her dashing maître d' husband who wore tight white pants that testified to his daily workouts at the gym. His black hair gleamed in a coiffure that didn't move. By American standards he looked gay. But Julie had learned that many European men looked gay by American standards of dress.

It was rumored that the chef had been offered an unheard of sum to cook for a famous restaurant in Rome, but had turned down the offer. Here stood the family's hand-wrought paradise, and pride could be seen in every blade of grass and table setting—too much so in some places, such as the gaudy lighting and the wine bottles decorating the high walls. But this was only a matter of taste; hard work and a spirit perfectionism had gone into the establishment.

Around nine o'clock, with lamps and candles lit, guests began to pour in through the gate, appetites piqued to breaking point. Julie and Umberto waved to Carolina and Elio and headed across the garden to their reserved table, where the glamorous maître d' was greeting Elio with an affectionate hug—their dinner would be gratis, on the house. Carolina, stunning with coiffed auburn hair, flowing summer dress, dazzling jewelry, and gold sandals introduced Dottore Gradi, who was a retired doctor from the village. He bowed over Julie's hand with the gracious reserve of the upper class. Julie noted that Carolina had invited her support team to the dinner; the people who regularly served as her buffer to Elio, who savagely ripped into her at every opportunity. He was a public health official who made rounds, so that often he was at home venting his angst on Carolina. Everyone in the Sabina knew about his confrontational personality—many had experienced it—and everyone felt sorry for Carolina and tried to be there for her. She was stuck for the time being because of her adolescent twins. Before becoming a public health administrator, Elio had been a mercenary in one of the African wars. The military training showed in him—a hard body with the belt fastened extra tight around his waist and the shirt tucked in as if cemented in place. Always tense, he couldn't meet others' eyes for long and his head flicked to his left shoulder continually, as if a nervous tic. Even when he battled adversaries in a conversation, his head would flick away to deliver his vituperative remarks. Julie could imagine Carolina falling in love with Elio's young good looks and air of authority, and having little idea of the intense verbal abuse that would surface later on. Her supporters at the table that evening were the ones who tolerated Elio because they had enough sympathy to pity him a bit. After all, he suffered inside for alienating everyone, though he did have one friend from the gym. And the two of them continued to speak in warm amiable voices, patting each other's arms with brotherly caring. Surely they harbored a secret love, Julie thought observing them.

At Carolina's urging, they seated themselves around the table, with Elio at one end facing Dr. Gradi, who sat next to Julie, with Umberto on her left at the head of the table. Carolina sat to his left, facing Julie. The distribution was perfect—Elio would have to make an effort to talk to anyone besides Dr. Gradi, or his loathed wife Carolina.

They got back up when the dazzling maître d' offered to take them on a private tour of the buffet room before the doors opened to the public. In the large, spic-and-span room, two long tables displayed thirty traditional dishes, all familiar to the Italians but not all of them to Julie. Family members—aunts, cousins—stood behind the tables in white coats and caps to serve the food that needed cutting, such as eggplant parmesan. At several smaller tables, young men in tuxedos carved prosciutto and *porchetta*, roasted pig.

They no sooner returned to their table than the band's leader welcomed the crowd and invited them to the buffet. The madhouse began—even the stoutest legs moved swiftly to the banquet room. The lure of food, and such anticipated homecooking, cut the cord of dignity. Julie made her selection of dishes, noting that the Italians went straight for the *supplí*, Roman fritters or croquettes, which she hadn't taken herself because of their calories. But now, seeing that the plump brown rolls represented a mandatory appetizer, she plucked a juicy *supplí* from the tray. When her plate was completely full, fuller than Thanksgiving dinner, she returned to the table, amazed to find that Umberto had fit far more food onto his plate. In the meantime, waiters had left two kinds of water and red and white wine bottles on each table.

Julie watched guests bring heaping plates back to their tables. The delight of feasting was in the air. There was no restaurant in the States similar to an Italian restaurant simply because the American and Italian food cultures were different. The Italians came to restaurants intending to gorge, slowly and plentifully over the course of several hours, the object of the evening being a communal enjoyment of food, its quality. The Americans dined out to enjoy eating *and drinking* as a social-life activity. When the meal ended, the Americans paid the bill and left, eager to move on to the next thing, even if home and bed. They also felt guilty, even ashamed, for overindulgence, for "pigging out." Perhaps it was a vestige of their Calvinist beginnings. The Italians were different. They came to eat with uninhibited joy. Then they relaxed so the food could digest, and perhaps that is where as a culture they learned their habit of gab. As a majority, they were content to sit at the table for hours, as if time and the world outside had disappeared. In the farming towns near Rome, people knew how to ballroom dance, and that would add to the long convening, the fun. It might also aid digestion for the dancers. Other *digestivi* were purported to help digestion—delicious homemade liqueurs from nuts, berries, fruit, and vegetables. Almost everyone in the garden had a thick midriff. The younger guests hadn't feasted long enough to add that layer, but their flesh was plump and headed toward midlife stoutness.

Julie turned to Umberto, "I've decided that after thousands of years, the Italians are genetically programmed to fit in a ton of food. I mean, their bodies are prepared for it. Mine isn't."

"Yes, it seems they have no problem making so much food disappear without a sign of discomfort in their faces."

"It must date back to the Romans—their successful conquests and luxurious lifestyle that followed."

"We eat too much," Elio grumbled from his corner of the table. He was the only Italian present with ascetic portions on his plate. He was a master of self-discipline, a zealot for regimen.

"On the other hand, all of the death notices that go up show people living into their eighties," Julie said.

"Yes, except for Vincente," Carolina said.

Everyone murmured sadly. The poster announcing his death that week had shown only thirty-eight years, for he had shot himself.

"The world is full of strife, it never ends," Dr. Gradi observed. "I've lived through a world war and how many Italian governments?"

"Dottore Gradi is from one of the oldest families in Collediana," Carolina said to Julie and Umberto. "He lives in the same family *palazzo* from 1400!"

"And it was a different world back then. The popes—often elected from noble families who vied for the privilege—gave their cardinals and bishops land and power in these hills and the farmers and artisans paid taxes and were kept poor," Dr. Gradi said.

"Who had Monte Donato?" Julie asked.

"Nicolò Boccamazzi—reviled by all. Bonifacio VIII's right-hand man."

"Julie lives on Monte Donato," Carolina said.

"So I've heard. You're the new keeper of the best view in town," he smiled. "Perhaps you'd be interested in a story about Cardinal Boccamazzi and the pope."

"Yes—"

"We'd all be interested," Carolina piped in.

"Well, it's long and complicated so I will make it short and simple."

They all smiled at him and nodded, except for Elio who ate with his head bent as if uninterested.

"Seven hundred years ago, around 1300, Bonifacio forced the Roman nobility to give all their southern lands to his nephew, Pietro Caetani. Around the same time, he gave his cardinal, Nicolò Boccamazzi, Monte Donato. The Orsinis and Savellis also did well everywhere in these parts. But Bonifacio's seizure of castles and land caused a rebellion, led particularly by the famous Colonna family. The pope was happily enjoying a feast much like this one to celebrate his new acquisitions when the rebels attacked his palace in Anagni."

"In the Monti Ernici," Carolina whispered across the table to Julie.

Dr. Gradi nodded. "*Allora,* the Frenchman Nogaret was with the partisans. Everyone knew that the pope intended to excommunicate the French king Filippo il Bello. Thus the Colonna faction waved the French flag as they made their attack, shouting, 'Long Live King Filippo! Death to the Pope!' They took Bonifaccio prisoner and made their demands: his abdication and restitution of the lands he had seized. Of course the pope refused. He pleaded with the townspeople to come to his rescue, but they sided with the rebels. Even his own servants and cardinals abandoned him, including Boccamazzi. Colonna's troops sacked the palace. Back in Rome, church forces mobilized and a cardinal was sent to Anagni to beg the people to save their blessed father, and this time the citizens rallied. They attacked the palace, freed the pope, and forced the rebels to flee."

"Did the pope give back the lands?" Julie asked.

"The poor pope lost his mind as a result of the insurgency and died within days. He may have been poisoned by his own inner circle because of his insanity. Who knows."

"How could he just take other people's possessions and give them to his family and cohorts?"

"It was a way of life back then—power, greed, usurpation. There was no system of checks and balances. Corruption was rampant. Family members killed other family members for money and land—sometimes for lust."

"We've hardly changed," Elio sneered from his corner. "The church is still corrupt, and worse, hypocritical!"

"I dare say you're right," Dr. Gradi conceded, "but perhaps we aren't quite so primitive as back then."

"Hmmf," Elio grunted.

"Who killed for lust?" Julie asked.

"Oh, I don't know. Let me think. We've had so many patricides, matricides, and fratricides among the nobility that they all blend together. Ah, here's an example—the Massimo brothers. They murdered their stepmother, Euphrosyne, to save the family honor. As you know, family honor has deep roots in Italy."

"Oh, yes," Umberto chimed in, "as does church involvement in state affairs."

"There's no excuse for it," Dr. Gradi shook his head.

"Have you read my Web site?" Elio growled.

"What happened?" Julie asked.

"Well, the brothers' widowed father, Lelio Massimo, had married his best friend's mistress—that would be Euphrosyne. And the friend was Marcantonio Colonna—do you recognize the name? Yes, he was a later generation of that same illustrious family who had attacked the pope in Anagni. Only now, it was the 1500s."

"The Colonnas still live in their palace in Rome," Carolina told Julie. "I'll show you one day."

"Yes, it still stands, but of course it has changed over the centuries. At any rate, Marcantonio Colonna was in his late forties on a mission to Sicily, where he fell madly in love with a young newlywed named Euphrosyne. First, he had her husband murdered by bandits, then he used his church connections to imprison and murder her father-in-law who had sought justice. That freed Marcantonio to bring his new mistress back to Rome. Soon enough, however, the bishop who had helped him with his scheme in exchange for political favors, summoned Marcantonio to Spain for failing to uphold his end of the bargain. Unfortunately, en route Marcantonio died. Someone poisoned him. Likely it was his best friend, Lelio Massimo, a member of the convoy, for immediately after, Lelio married Euphrosyne. His sons were outraged—everyone in Rome already knew about the murders of her husband and father-in-law, and now she was living under their roof, wed to their father. So they shot her, one bullet each, and then were beheaded by the pope to set an example for the nobility, whose killings had gotten out of control. I have a book you can borrow, if you're interested," Dr. Gradi finished.

"Yes, I want to borrow it," Julie said.

"And what do you think of your election?" Elio fired across the table. "Can Obama beat McCain?"

"I hope so, we have to end the Bush regime or we'll have another four years of destroying America."

"I watched the news, the Clintons at the convention. I detest the Clintons, but especially him!" Elio spat through his teeth at her and flicked his head to the side. Suddenly the table was a boxing ring with Elio and Julie inside.

"Yes," she said neutrally, "people either hate or love Bill Clinton."

"He's a big liar, and I don't mean about that woman in his

office, I mean Bosnia! He broke international law and made up lies about it. And look what he did to Rwanda. He let genocide happen! And it's obvious why—do I need to tell you?—he's racist! Bush is bad, I know, but he's much better than Clinton."

"What about Katrina? That was all about race," Julie said, unable to resist his bait.

Elio saw his predicament but was quick to rebound, "And I hate Kennedy! He started the Viet Nam War. And he attacked Cuba, but ha-ha, his plan didn't work out, did it? Ha-ha."

Umberto was digging in his pocket and pulled out a small Swiss army knife. He opened the little blade, "Here Julie, would you like to use this?"

Julie stared at the knife: does he mean for my fingernails? Are they dirty? Then she laughed, he meant for Elio. "Yes, in true Italian fashion."

Dr. Gradi's pleasant voice humorously remarked about the rampant corruption in Italian politics and the table settled down. Umberto put his knife away. Elio gave a raucous laugh and delivered a few derisive remarks about Berlusconi, to which the doctor replied in a similar jocular vein. Waiters briskly cleared the dinner plates, and the feasters in the scintillating garden turned their thoughts to dessert—*il dolce*—and what the banquet tables would offer. Couples got up and danced, all together in a long line that moved the points of a compass, so that onlookers from all sides of the garden could have a frontal view at least once.

Red wine was tumbling into Umberto's glass for the umpteenth time. Julie made a face at him, "You're the driver."

"What? You mean you're not going to drive my police car home for us?"

When she was young, Julie never thought about who would drive, but now she could truly imagine Umberto's bleary eyes trying to keep to the treacherously winding road, possibly meeting another inebriated, Saturday-night driver coming around the bend on the wrong side. With a sigh of resignation Umberto filled his water glass, "There, I'm going to start drinking water from now on. To please you."

"Grazie, Umberto."

Julie was keeping an eye on the doors to the banquet room. The minute she saw three people stream through, with others, multitudes, pushing back their chairs to join them and begin the stampede, she was up and making her own way to the desserts, with her table companions following her cue. Never in her life had she seen so many desserts, most in cake and lasagna pans, many with fruit toppings. She chose modest portions of several delectable confections and added a miniature cannolo. As she walked back to the table she marveled at all the happy guests around her heading the same way, their plates held out before them, piled high with mounds and mounds of cream and frosting. Umberto plopped down in his seat next to her, and she pretended not to notice he had one of those piled-high plates, so he noticed for her, "I've gone out of my mind, as you can see. It's sinful, sinful!" His one-quarter Italian blood allowed him to gorge, but his larger portion of Germanic genes made him repent. What was more amazing was how the next time she looked, his plate was scraped clean. At least he didn't smoke. But it seemed he might be paying for the evening's indiscretions for he made an abrupt departure for the restroom.

Dr. Gradi turned his elegant head to Julie and with a gallant smile invited her to dance. She accepted, not worrying about her ignorance of the polkas and mazurkas, because as a woman all she would have to do was inexpertly follow his lead. At eighty, Dr. Gradi was a sedate dancer, no speedy spins or backward thrusts, but his adept stepping to the music's rhythm and his firm control of her body gave her a thrill. They returned to their table flushed and satisfied to have enjoyed every detail of the evening from garden dining to dancing.

Suddenly, William was at her side, "Julie! I didn't know you were here until I saw you dancing. It's been months. Come on, give me a big hug!" And he pulled her completely against his body and held her so tight that he squeezed out the word she was thinking—"Gross!"—but he didn't hear it because of the music and voices around them. "Come on, Julie!" he said in her ear, "We both need hugs. You Americans invented free love."

"And prudery."

Carolina waved enthusiastically at him, "William! Where have you been hiding yourself? Sit down. What's your news? How's the house coming along?"

He took Umberto's chair and Julie reluctantly sat back down, stuck with William at her side. In everyday life, she tried to avoid him, never accepting his invitations to cocktails at his house and never visiting Bar Luna, where he was a regular on Friday and Saturday nights.

Quickly he shed Carolina and focused on Julie, "Why are you hiding yourself?"

She made a noncommittal face and shrugged her shoulders.

"When did we last see each other? Was it at Carlotta's? What an enchanted evening that was."

Yes, Carlotta's. Julie had been invited to Carlotta's exquisite eighteenth-century palace for a late afternoon swim in the small oval pool on a lushly planted terrace facing mountains. The palace wrapped one side of the hilltown, its rooms and gardens on several levels of the steep slope. In the 1980s, the owner, in need of cash for his profligate ways, had sold off segments of the building, and Carlotta's family had bought the largest portion.

While Julie floated in the water, her hostess, a beautiful brunette countess in her mid-forties, stood languidly on the sidelines in her bikini smoking a cigarette. It was impossible not to see at every turn her slinky, undernourished body that was the coveted emblem of high society. Carlotta had apartments in New York, Paris, and London, and in several hotspots in Italy. She had never married, and an invisible barbed-wire wall protected her from true intimacy.

"By the way," Carlotta said casually, blowing out smoke, "I've invited William for cocktails."

What! Julie's mind protested. An evening trapped with William?

"He'll be here any minute," Carlotta added blandly.

"Then I'd better change."

"You don't have to."

"I want to."

"Suit yourself. I'm going to stay like this," she said, but reached for a sheer swimsuit cover-up that came to her thigh and tied at the waist

Soon after, the three of them sat on lounge chairs while the sun finished setting and night came on. Julie had asked for juice, but Carlotta wouldn't hear of it, and laced her peach nectar with Prosecco. Then she and William proceeded to polish off two bottles of Prosecco. The only food served with the drinks had been olives and pistachios. After awhile Carlotta stood to smoke, and feeling loose, divulged her personal and troubled family relationships—her imperious mother who didn't care who Carlotta was as a person but only wanted to see her properly married, and her rival, backstabbing sister who had suggested she was a lesbian. Carlotta stood there poised like a statue as she revealed these deeply painful memories. After each revelation, she took a long sip of Prosecco, followed by a drag on her cigarette, while William filled the pause with his silken platitudes: "Your integrity's more important than your sister's malicious gossip. It's obvious she's jealous of her beautiful and talented sister."

Carlotta put down her glass to light another cigarette, which she inhaled deeply, as if it soothed her wounds. "But why? She has everything. A rich husband, two adorable children, a mansion in Mayfair, a summer home on the Côte d'Azur...."

"Perhaps she envies your independence and acumen for business, all your properties and collections. Do you have any plans for new acquisitions?"

The topic perked her up. "I was thinking as soon as I sell another Picasso, I'll upgrade in Paris," she said. "I've been spending more time there and my pied-à-terre—even though it's huge—isn't enough space."

"Then it's time to trade-in," William said.

Her glazed eyes came to rest on Julie before she bent to flick her ash into the silver ashtray on the small table cluttered with glasses, bottles, and appetizers.

"You know what, Julie, Loredana is selling her apartment on the ground floor—the one that used to be our stables. It's charming. She's fixed it up so nicely. It's perfect for you. Shall I ask Loredana to show it to you tomorrow?"

"I'm happy where I am."

"Really? It's so wild there and this apartment is finished and has all our gardens and ambiance surrounding it. Why don't we call her and take a look at it? Just for fun."

The drinking went on. Julie couldn't understand how that frail body of 100 pounds could handle so much alcohol. She had rung the servant for a third bottle. He was Sri Lankan, in his thirties, and wore blue jeans and a green livery coat. He had a good life there living in the multi-storied, treasure-filled palace, but he probably earned too little to strike out on his own. He was this era's equivalent of an indentured servant, Julie thought, and wondered what he was thinking when he delivered another bottle and swept away the empties.

Carlotta swayed a bit with half-closed eyes—she had reached that state of drunken oblivion that Julie remembered from college days. The brain twirled rather deliciously while all the senses, and the ego, screamed to be touched in a satisfying way, which was ultimately unattainable.

She spoke now, with her half-filled Prosecco glass dangling precariously from her right hand. "I'm a countess, I'm a countess." It was a proud, righteous statement, but also tinged with anger and frustration.

"That you are," William purred from his lounge chair, gazing up at her as if she were a goddess.

"I'm a countess, that's who I am, every fiber of me."

Too good for the rest of us, Julie finished silently for her.

But William voiced it as praise, "You're a countess and heads above the rest of us. Don't let anyone ever forget it."

The night enveloped them with the shimmering and romantic evanescence of the elite, who had lived separately and royally down through the ages. The vast blue-black sky over pristine mountains had become magical with stars and made the oval pool gleam with luscious enticement. The palace's parapets and steep terraces of lemon trees and other horticulture decorated with ancient urns set the stage for tantalizing romance that might occasionally happen but never in the fulfilling way suggested by the luxurious and aesthetic ambiance, for it was not within the human organism to sustain such unrealities.

Carlotta excused herself to go to the poolside cabana. William got up ostensibly for a handful of nuts, but as soon as he had them he leaned casually over Julie's lounge chair, his sour lips hovering just above hers, "How about a kiss?" She turned away in revulsion, knowing full well he would never dare such a move with Carlotta. And really, did he believe she wanted his kiss?

And now he was at her side at the end-of-summer party. Who had invited him? He certainly got around. His honey-silken voice prattled on at her side as if she had never rejected him. "Of course I've been away all month—England. That's the damn trouble with us expats—we're always coming and going." He was smiling at her with far too much familiarity. "You look so lovely tonight, Julie, your dress, the earrings—," he lightly fingered her hair, "and your hair—so shiny."

She drew away; she was not an enticing young thing. He was reciting his standard lines to melt women, what women? "It's been a dry summer here," she said flatly, "bad for the olives but wonderful for people—the weather's been divine."

"Yes, indeed. And it's sure to last a few more weeks. We'll have to plan some picnics. I know a few good spots." He rested his hand on her thigh and tested her out with a few rubs that moved her dress above her knee.

Julie stared at her lap briefly and then looked him in the eye, "What are you doing?"

His hand drew back and he laughed charmingly, "Have no fear, you have nothing to worry about with me."

"But you do have something to worry about with me," Umberto said to him, suddenly towering, with his full two hundred and twenty pounds at William's side, "because you're occupying my place at the table."

William got up, a kind of lazy cat's stretch, "Oh, how are you, Umberto? Still putting out your tabloid? I was just leaving."

"Lucky thing."

"Let's talk this week, Julie," William said airily, as if he owned her.

Julie watched the transfer of men in the chair next to her. Umberto's weight was cumbersome and he more or less crash-landed. It made her think that at his house he had a few broken chairs put aside.

Not long after, the band's leader thanked everyone for coming and the party ended. The police car headed home. Julie watched every bend in the road, but Umberto drove accurately, if a bit jerkily, but the jerks were the vehicle not the man, for the ride to the restaurant had been the same. Umberto's spirit had as much gustiness as the jeep, and he treated her to a stream of his eclectic experiences, whether true or false.

"And besides being the honorary consul for Albania in Switzerland, I was Italy's minister of foreign affairs for Serbia. The Italian government was up in arms when they heard about that posting. They claimed it was fake, illegal."

"Where was your office?"

"Right in my home. It was a short-lived position. I didn't

want to take on the Italians—Aldo Moro is a good example of what can happen if you thwart the government."

Julie laughed. "What about the honorary consulship in Switzerland? How long did you do that?"

"Three months. I resigned after that."

"But what did you do? What were your obligations?"

"Nothing at all," he laughed. "And did I tell you I'm a count?"

"Yes, you tell me every time we meet. One of your cronies in the Balkans drew up paperwork and now you're a count."

"Exactly."

"But why did you want to be a count?"

"The title comes in handy."

"But how? You weren't born that way, it's just a piece of paper, and everyone knows you arranged it."

"But I like it—it tickles me to be officially a count. And besides, in the beginning, no one was born a count. They all bought their titles from the Church."

"Or they were priests who got promoted and upgraded their families."

"Sometimes I think that was my true calling. But it's too late now. I'm only sorry I no longer have direct access to the pope."

"Why not?"

"Because of my reporting. I've been blacklisted. But is it my fault certain priests phone me to tell me their grievances?"

"No, as long as they aren't just playing office politics."

"That's unavoidable, but my instincts tell me when to trust their information. But the real cleavage came in the eighties. Did I ever tell you my Cuba story?"

"I'm going to need paper and pen. That's the only way I'll be able to piece together your enormous puzzle."

"Good, that makes me feel important."

"You are. You're a count. So what happened in Cuba?"

"I went on a private mission—sanctioned by the pope's first secretary, though no one had authorized him to do so. It was an idea we cooked up together. I was supposed to gauge Castro's interest in having a visit from the pope, not just a quick stopover, but the real thing, two to three days of highly publicized visits to the Madonnas in Havana and El Cobre."

He laughed with glee and gassed down the rocky slope and across the dry ford, swerving hard to the left to come up neatly on the other side. "Whee! I love that!" he said. "Anyhow, our scheme took a lot of planning and eventually I went off to Havana under the auspices of a British radio station that had a Cuban contact in the government. I waited for days in my hotel to be contacted but nothing happened. Realizing the plan might fail and I would return home empty-handed, I wrote a letter to the Swiss Embassy stating my mission and including the pope's wish list for Cuba, which included making Christmas a holiday again. I knew the Cuban secret police would intercept my letter and therefore find out I was waiting to meet Castro on behalf of the pope, even though the pope had no idea about the mission."

"*Macché!*" Julie said incredulously.

"I swear all of this is true. I lived it."

"But to represent the pope when you hadn't been authorized—"

"That was the thrill of it! Everything took careful planning, foresight. I had to be sure my new plan would work, so I photocopied my letter before I sent it, and hand-delivered the photocopy to the embassy, since I knew the original would never reach them. Unfortunately, that part of my plan backfired, because the embassy got extremely angry at my misuse of diplomacy. Nevertheless, the pope's wish list reached Castro's authorities, and on my last day in the country they abducted me to an empty villa."

"Who abducted you?"

"The secret police. They interrogated me for hours. I kept telling them that everything about my mission was clearly and honestly described my letter to the Swiss ambassador. Finally they put me on a plane home."

"Lucky you didn't mysteriously disappear."

"But I am a sincere friend of Cuba!" he bleated.

"Was that the end of it?"

"Not quite. The Cuban diplomats in Rome began asking the Vatican about the purpose of my visit." He chortled. "The Holy See insisted they knew nothing about it, which was true—the secretary and I had hatched the plan in complete secrecy. And the Vatican was fully aware of the Reagan administration's total opposition to a papal visit and didn't want to go near such a sensitive issue, even if the pope really wanted to visit Cuba, which he did."

"So it all fizzled out."

"More or less. But first I got called into the Cuban embassy for a thorough interrogation, where I convinced them that purely good will had been the intent of my mission. But years later, when the pope finally visited Cuba, I was denied a visa to enter the country." He chuckled. "I was disappointed, but not surprised."

"What about the secretary?"

"Oh, he managed to save himself with convincing lies."

"And then you published the whole story."

"Not then, much later, after the pope made it to Cuba. I had to take some credit for paving the way. After all, I paid with my career—I was henceforth outlawed from the Vatican."

With more chuckles, he pulled into his quiet courtyard where his white cat sat on a table by the front door.

"This has been a wonderful evening. Thank you, Umberto."

"Same." They pecked cheeks and agreed to see each other soon. Friday pizzas had become a routine, as long as Umberto wasn't traveling.

Julie got in her car and drove home taking the curves with lazy contentment. She vowed to eat only fresh fruit and salad the following day. That was the way her eating habits had become living in Italy: eat as little as possible most of the time because big dinners were just around the bend. Congregating with friends to eat plentifully happened several times a week.

The next morning, the last day of August, Julie climbed Monte Donato's summit behind her house. She passed the igloolike mounds of earth covering rooms to former dwellings, some with cavelike openings revealing dark interiors with stone foundations. People had lived there. She passed through a high arch, the best-preserved relic of the ruins, and obviously repaired with fresh cement some years before. Few people explored beyond the arch because the going was rough—precipitous, rocky, slippery, and overgrown with thorns. But for those who persevered, the best treasure awaited, a jutting stone parapet offering the full Sabina panorama to the west. Julie gained her position, and rested her elbows on the thousand-year-old wall. She had first noticed it during one of her walks in the valley, looking up at the hilltop, but it had taken her months of scrabbling through the woods to find the white wall. Long before Monte Donato's destruction in 1307, a portion of the castle had risen here and may have served as a watchtower for the western sweep of land. She wondered from which direction the Colledianians had attacked Monte Donato. Dr. Gradi might know. She would invite him over for coffee, and if he was still sure-footed enough, she would lead him here, for she felt certain he—an aristocrat—hadn't discovered the spot in youth, for only the rough hunters combed the mountainsides so thoroughly. The elite took *passeggiate* along picturesque lanes. But he might know if her house was the only survivor of that terrible sacking and burning seven hundred years before. She liked to think her house had been a shepherd's simple dwelling, because of the cave inside the living room, now covered by a modern door.

The landscape, its history, mesmerized her. Learning about her place, the Sabina, and Rome's historic authority over the territory had become her life, her passion, though she also knew that one day she would leave, return to her own land and family, even if her whole being felt more at home in Italy. She could accept living there for the rest of her days as an outsider, an ex-pat, a mere observer who made international friends and was part of a hybrid community. But something deeper existed, and living here among the farmers and villagers had shown her that the only fragment of solace in an individual's solitary life was family, that unclassifiable love. A piece of her was missing without it, even if one day it broke her heart to say goodbye to all she loved here.

The glorious valley rustled gently in the cool morning air, the distant rows of olives not yet casting shadows. She gazed with the sublimity of it all filling her, steeping her in the past generations upon generations of lives and eyes that had inhabited this ancient land and hill before her. The past embodied her like fluid, like time immemorial, and she knew that she, too, was a brief flicker there, a presence on Monte Donato, her place forever etched in its continuum.